Gillian Linscott's journalistic career has ranged from reporting chip-pan fires in Bootle to street riots in Belfast. Her previous incarnations include civil servant, market gardener, playwright and parliamentary radio reporter.

She lives in a cottage in Herefordshire with her husband – also a writer – and enjoys skiing, riding and hill-walking. Exotic locations and off-beat, first-hand research are characteristic of her books, the first of which was set in a French nudist colony.

Her tenth whodunnit, *Widow's Peak*, is the fourth to feature the suffragette sleuth Nell Bray, a detective heroine who has already acquired a large and loyal following.

GILLIAN LINSCOTT

Widow's Peak

WARNER FUTURA

A *Warner Futura* Book

First published in Great Britain in 1994
by Little, Brown and Company
This edition published by Warner Futura in 1995

A CIP catalogue record for this book
is available from the British Library.

ISBN 0 7515 1356 3

Printed in England by Clays Ltd, St Ives plc

Warner Futura
A Division of
Little, Brown and Company (UK)
Brettenham House
Lancaster Place
London WC2E 7EN

The author would like to thank the Thomas Cook Archive in London and Thérèse Robache of the Musée Alpin in Chamonix. Also especial thanks to mountain guide Dave Cumming, who gave invaluable advice on dealing with crevasses, both in fact and fiction.

Widow's Peak

ONE

THE FIRST THING I KNEW about it was a chipping sound from somewhere higher up. I was lying, eyes closed and more than half asleep, on a strip of grass starred with the orange flowers of mountain arnica between the pinewoods and the blue-green ice of the glacier. A couple of mad-eyed goats that had shared my lunch of bread and plums were tip-toeing around, hoping for more. The sun was spreading the warm scent of the pines but under it the ice gave off something that wasn't quite a scent, more of a freshness that went straight to the heart and brain. A long way above, and out of sight from where I was lying, the summit of Mont Blanc would still be deep in snow, even in high summer. I let it all soak into me, glad that I was there, even if it did amount to something like desertion.

It had been a spur-of-the-moment decision to come to Chamonix. On Wednesday 13 July 1910, I'd been pacing my living-room in Hampstead in a fury that I knew would only be soothed by throwing a bucketful of something unpleasant over the Home Secretary or getting myself out of the country until the temptation had passed. The evening before in the House of Commons an unholy alliance of time-serving Liberals and Tory backwoodsmen had smothered the bill that would have given the vote to women at last. Months of discussion and lobbying and self-restraint had gone for nothing. We'd even stopped marching and demonstrating for six months so as to give negotiations a fair chance. We'd been duped. I could feel my arm muscles tensing into brick-throwing mode.

In the end, of the two courses open to me, I decided for

1

once on the one that wouldn't land me in prison. I drew all my money out of the bank, spent most of it on a second-class return ticket to Chamonix and rooted out my climbing boots and ice-axe from the back of the cupboard. I deliberately travelled alone. Friends slow you down and I'd been in a hurry to get away. Anyway, I'd be bad company for anybody until I got my temper back. I arrived in Chamonix on the Saturday, found a cheap pension in the unfashionable part of town near the station, spread out my old maps on the bed and planned a campaign of walks to re-introduce myself to a part of the world that had been familiar to me a long time ago.

The Glacier des Bossons was an obvious route for the second day. It dominates the town and the whole valley almost more than the summit of Mont Blanc itself, pouring itself down in an immense frozen waterfall between the rounded Dôme du Goûter and the sharp point of the Aiguille du Midi. It hangs so steeply over the town that at any second you expect it to lose its hold on the rocks and slip and shatter over the valley, chiming like a million crashing chandeliers, obliterating hotels and cafés and shops selling dried edelweiss and carved chamois in a great crystal avalanche. From a distance the ice-blocks on its lower reaches look as small as children's building bricks, but when you get close to them each one is two or three times the height of a person. They nudge each other down the mountain so slowly that only delicate scientific instruments can catch them moving at all, so relentlessly that they could crush large buildings like cud in a cow's teeth.

At first I thought the chipping sound was stones rattling down inside the glacier as the ice melted, but it was too regular for that. Too loud for a bird, although there were plenty of those chit-chitting away in the woods. Then I heard voices too from up above, several men speaking French. I concentrated and recognised the local accent.

'What is it?'

'I've found his boot.'

'Leave it and come over here. We're going to try lifting him.'

2

It sounded as if some tourist had wandered off on his own across the glacier and come to grief. In case I could be of any use I packed my things and hurried up the path. Two or three hairpin bends further up I was on a level with the rescue party. There were more men than I expected, five or six of them, with two in the broad-brimmed felt hats of the Chamonix guides. They were on the edge of the glacier not far from the path, clustered round something. One of the guides broke away from the group and came towards me.

'I'm sorry, madam, but you shouldn't come any further.'

He was quite tall, probably in his early forties. His face was tanned, with a prominent nose and very clear grey eyes that met mine, straight and level. He was polite but not deferential, as you'd expect from a guide. Self-assured everywhere as a profession, they tend to be arrogant in Chamonix. He'd guessed my nationality and spoken careful English. I asked him in French if there'd been an accident and if I could be of any help.

'An accident, yes, but I'm afraid there's nothing we can do except bring him down.'

It struck me that his attitude towards a fatality was a touch off-hand, even allowing for a guide's contempt for tourists who commit stupidities.

'The accident was many years ago, madam. I think this poor man has been on his way down for a long time.'

'On his way down?'

He gestured towards the summit of Mont Blanc.

'If a man dies up there and his body is not recovered it must come down the glacier in the course of time. It may take thirty years, even forty, but down he must come sooner or later.'

Glaciers flow like rivers only much more slowly. I imagined layers of incautious or unlucky Victorian climbers, still up there waiting their turn.

'Pierre, can you bring the other rope?'

A shout from the group on the ice. Pierre gave me a long look and came to a decision.

'Would you like to see him? He's probably English. Quite a lot of them are.'

3

I decided that after thirty years or more it was mountaineering history rather than simple ghoulishness and followed him. The other men looked startled at first but were too preoccupied to worry about me. They were entirely matter-of-fact about their work. To guides and porters it was no news that Mont Blanc killed people. One of them stood back to let me look at him. He was lying in a shallow trough of ice, probably the remains of a crevasse. Half of his left leg was gone and his right arm either torn away by the glacier or twisted out of sight underneath him. The capriciousness of the grinding ice had left his face almost unharmed. His beard, brown and square cut, and his bushy sideburns might have come fresh from the barber's. His hair was brown too, quite long and drawn back from the face. His eyelids were closed and his skin, yellowish-brown like a mummy's, was stretched tight over his cheekbones. There was a deep gash in his forehead, gaping open above the closed eyes. He was still wearing breeches, jacket and waistcoat and the remains of a shirt, but the clothes had been torn away from his right side, exposing crushed and yellowed ribs with leathery skin clinging to them. On the other side his gold watch-chain trailed.

'What happened to his forehead?' I said.

Pierre looked down at the gash and its exposed edges of bone.

'We think that might have been done by his own ice-axe. He was probably holding it when he went into a crevasse or got caught by an avalanche.'

'Yes, I've heard of that happening. Why do you think he might be English?'

'There's a look about him.'

I could see what he meant. Even with parts of his body missing, there was still a solid and four-square look about the man. His brow and shoulders were broad, the quality of his tweed jacket good. Very much the young Victorian on holiday.

'When was he found?'

'Yesterday, by some children looking for berries. We've

4

been trying to cut him free of the ice all morning.'

They were completing the process as I watched. Ropes, doubled up, were passed under his shoulders and back. A few last blows with an ice-axe cut his jacket free and he was lifted quite gently by the guides and porters, but with no particular reverence, on to a heavy stretcher of wood and leather waiting beside the path. As they let it down the body tilted slightly. In a flash of gold a watch slithered out of its fob pocket. It fell at my feet and almost without thinking I picked it up and opened the cover. As I'd hoped, there was an inscription inside.

To Arthur Mordiford,
*   On the occasion of attaining his twenty-first birthday,*
from his loving father and mother. 22 February 1875.

'You're right. He was British.'
The guide Pierre glanced at me.
'What name?'
I handed the watch to him.
'Arthur Mordiford.'
I pronounced it carefully, thinking the name would be strange to him, and was amazed by the change in his face. He looked as if somebody had hit him hard in the stomach. I glanced round at the other men but they were busy strapping the body on to the stretcher and the name seemed to have no effect on them. There was one exception. The other guide was an older man and he was looking at Pierre and nodding slowly to himself. To give Pierre time to recover I asked the older guide if he'd known Arthur Mordiford.

'I never met him, but I remember the accident. Thirty years ago. He went into a crevasse by the Grands Mulets rocks.'

He lowered his voice and glanced across at Pierre. We couldn't see his face. He was kneeling by the stretcher, checking what the porters were doing.

'Pierre Martin's father was his guide. He was killed too.'
'That's Pierre Martin?'

I glanced towards the group by the stretcher. He nodded and gave me a look that said it would be best to keep quiet.

'Are we ready? We'll take it in turns carrying him.'

Pierre Martin slipped the watch back into the fob pocket. He didn't look at me or the older guide. There was a tension about the group now. They'd sensed his need to get it over with. When one of their party made a last check of where the body had been lying and came back with his hands full, they were impatient with him.

'I still can't get that boot out.'

'Stop worrying about the boot. We want to get him down.'

'But his foot might be . . .'

'Never mind that. He won't be needing it again.'

'In that case I might as well throw these back in the glacier. He won't be needing them either.'

He was carrying an ice-axe, its long shaft broken and splintered, and a small oblong package in oilskin covering. He began to unwrap it.

'Looks like a book, with handwriting. Probably his diary.'

He opened it at random then shrugged, up against the barrier of a foreign language. He puzzled over it for a while, then handed it to me. The others were too busy to mind. I glanced at the page he'd opened. Although the edges of the book were buffed and tattered, the waterproof covering had done its work and the ink was fresh and black on the lined page. It was curly copperplate handwriting, very much that of an educated man, and went with the good tweeds and the gold watch.

We are camped here on a stony meadow, with the town spread out below us and the glaciers and the great peaks above. Our expedition at rest has the air of a picnic party. One of the guides, Antoine, is preparing our evening meal of soup, cold fowl, ham and asparagus. Tom has insisted on celebrating the start of our venture by breaking out two of the six bottles of champagne reserved for our arrival at the summit. We made an impressive party as we left our lodgings this morning . . .

6

Four of the porters had shouldered the stretcher with its wrapped bundle and were looking at Pierre Martin, waiting for the signal to move off. I closed the book, wrapped it up hastily and gave it to him. I'd have liked to have read more, but I had no claim to it and he seemed to be the leader of the retrieval party. He hesitated before putting out his hand to take it and looked at me. There was such sadness in his eyes that I felt my own hand moving to touch his arm in consolation and had to restrain it, though what exactly I'd be consoling him for I didn't know.

'Thank you for what you're doing, Monsieur Martin.'

As if this unfortunate Victorian were somehow my responsibility, just because we'd shared a language.

He nodded, said good afternoon then turned to give the signal to the stretcher-bearers. As they moved off the others fell in behind them, Pierre at the back. He was carrying two ice-axes, his own and the broken one that had come down with Arthur Mordiford, and the journal bulged in the pocket of his jacket.

From further up the path I looked down and saw the procession below me. They were approaching a party of tourists on their way up, probably coming for tea and a view of the glacier from the terrace of the Chalet du Cerro. Some were on mules and others on foot, a wavering line of white panamas and pastel-coloured sunshades. As the two parties came close I watched the advance of hats and parasols check itself and form into little agitated clumps on either side of the path. Slowly the stretcher and its burden were carried down between them. Not the way that Arthur Mordiford would have imagined his descent from Mont Blanc thirty years ago. I went on with my walk and decided to put it out of my mind. Whoever he'd been and whatever puzzles he might have left, it was no business of mine.

TWO

I KEPT THAT RESOLUTION FOR eight days and six hours. In that time I forgot Arthur Mordiford almost entirely in the course of what turned out to be an unexpectedly good holiday. In the years I'd been away from Chamonix, tourism had been kind to it and it had become fashionable, with more shops and cafés and grand hotels. The result was that a fair part of London stayed there for the summer, and although three-quarters of it was made up of the kind of people I'd come away to avoid, it included a few old friends and walking acquaintances from years back. We made up parties and spent long days walking in the mountains. We got ambitious, bought an Alpine Club rope and tackled, with varying success, some of the easier rock climbs. We swam in freezing cold mountain lakes and restored our circulation with bottles of the cheap local wine, brewed coffee on wood fires, slept out one night in a herdsman's hut.

Admittedly, part of the pleasure of this Bohemian way of life was how much it scandalised the more respectable holidaymakers down in the valley, the kind who thought they were taking a big risk on a mule-ride to the Mer de Glace. Unchaperoned mixed walking parties were regarded by some of them as a sign of the breakdown of civilisation. When an interfering person raised the point we told her that we were perfectly prepared to take some suitably elderly matron along with us, provided she didn't mind being dragged up near-vertical rock faces on a tight rope. When this produced no volunteers, we went our unrespectable way. A woman friend and myself got tired

8

of climbing in skirts and had breeches made. The form was that we left town in our skirts, to avoid causing shock to the timid, changed into our breeches at the first empty hut we came to and stowed the skirts in a corner, for retrieval on the way down.

One afternoon, coming down from a good day, we saw another woman in breeches swinging along the path in front of us at a good pace, on her own. She wore a battered felt hat, like a smaller version of the mountain guides', and beneath it her hair was as silver as snow under the moon.

'That's Easyday,' one of my friends said when I drew his attention to her. 'She's a bit of a legend round here.'

' "Easyday"?'

'Yes. You know – An Easy Day for a Lady.'

I did know. The phrase was notorious in climbing circles, denoting something too simple to be worth doing.

'What's her real name?'

'No idea. I've never spoken to her and whenever you see her she's usually disappearing rapidly into the distance, like today. She's lived up in a hut on the mountains as long as anybody can remember. The story is that she's a black sheep from some very distinguished English family. Can't remember what family, though.'

The felt hat and white hair were out of sight by then and we saw no more of Easyday on our walks. I was sorry about that, but everything else was very much to my satisfaction. After a week my hands and face were as brown as a Romany's, my temper was restored and I could think of the Home Secretary, Winston Churchill, without an urge to commit violence – or almost. Some of my friends were determined to climb Mont Blanc and were planning to hire guides and porters and have a try. It had been an ambition of mine since I'd first set eyes on it as a child, more than twenty years before, and I wanted very much to be one of the party. The problem was that attempts on Mont Blanc are costly – around 250 francs or ten pounds in sterling – and I was rapidly running out of money. Even lunching off bread and cheese and dining off omelettes and small *pichets* of wine in the cheaper cafés, my stock of

9

francs was dwindling. If I was careful I had just about enough to last until the end of the week, but after that it would be the train back to London, leaving my friends to climb Mont Blanc without me.

I was brooding on this late one afternoon as a crowd of us were sitting round a table outside the Pâtisserie des Alpes. It was the time of day when walking and climbing parties that had started at first light were back down in the valley, planting their booted feet under café tables, spreading their maps over the tops of them and re-living every step and tight place of the day. The parties that had guides always brought them to the café and treated them deferentially. A word of praise from a guide, even the admission that the group hadn't been as much trouble as expected, was something that everyone angled for shamelessly. Now and again at these café sessions I'd glance round to see if I could spot Pierre Martin, but although there were plenty of grey eyes and prominent noses under guides' hats, none of them belonged to him.

Waitresses in black dresses and white aprons stepped lightly among haversacks, ice-axes and coils of ropes, bearing trays of coffee and cream cakes. Scraps of conversation drifted, some in French and German but mostly in confident English, with loud braying laughter.

'. . . had to haul him up on the rope. Don't believe he touched the rock all the way up, then when he got to the top he said . . .'

'There was a German party last year that did it in three hours and twenty minutes and that was without guides.'

'. . . so I said to him, you've dropped your *what* in the crevasse? I mean, of all the things to take up a mountain with you . . .'

'Keep still, everybody. Jeremy's taking a photograph.'

I leaned back in my chair, staring up at the mountains and trying to fix it all in my mind for when I'd be back in London. Chair legs scraped.

'I'm sorry.'

'Not at all. My fault entirely. Had a good day?'

A cheerful-looking man with bright eyes and a neat

10

beard was sitting at a table behind me. From the number of coffee cups on the table it looked as if he might have been part of a group and the others had left.

'A very good day, thank you. We went up to the Jardin de Talèfre.'

That was one of the good things about Chamonix. If you bothered to introduce yourself at all it was in terms of what you'd climbed, not who you were.

'Jolly good. Or I'm sure it would be if I had the slightest idea where it was.'

He was wearing light holiday tweeds but didn't look like a climber or walker, with none of the tan that comes from even a few days in the mountains.

'Have you just arrived?'

'We got here on Friday, but I haven't had much chance to look round yet.'

Early thirties. Tending to plumpness, but with an active look about him. Full red lips above the beard, an air of finding life amusing. My own party were beginning to break up and disperse to their various pensions.

'See you tomorrow then, Nell? First train to Montenvers.'

I waved goodbye to them and began to fold up my map.

'Show me where you were today.'

An invitation no walker can refuse. I showed him and found that two more coffees had arrived.

'You'll have a coffee with me? I should have introduced myself. My name's Hector Tenby.'

I told him my name. Since he'd bought me coffee it was only civil to drink it, although I didn't intend to spend any more of my precious holiday with a man who didn't even know where the Talèfre glacier was.

'I gather you've met my Uncle Arthur.'

I stared at him over the cup, puzzled. It rang no bells.

'What's your uncle's other name?'

A pause.

'Mordiford.'

I must have looked taken aback, I suppose, because he was instantly apologetic.

11

'I say, I'm sorry. I shouldn't have sprung it on you like that. It can't have been a nice experience at all.'

His brow was furrowed, lips parted.

'I've just realised. You reminded me of somebody. You're like him.'

It was his turn to be surprised and mine to be apologetic.

'After thirty years in the ice I shouldn't have thought . . .'

'The face shape, I think, or possibly the hair. More of an impression than anything.'

A kind of four-square confidence about his place in the world. That was what had struck me, looking at the body in its ice-cradle.

'He's recognisable then?'

'Yes. His head's almost undamaged but . . .'

I was thinking of the gash in the forehead. He leaned towards me across the table.

'Miss Bray, if you're concerned about upsetting me, please don't be. I was three years old when my uncle died, and my mother had never been close to her brothers in any case. He was just a name and a story to me. But for reasons I'll explain, it would be very helpful to me if I knew something about the condition of his body. If you feel up to it, that is.'

'How did you know I was there?'

He smiled.

'It's a gossipy little town this, isn't it? And Uncle is rather the story of the week.'

Down in the valley I supposed that was the case, but I'd spent most of my time up the mountains. Hector Tenby leaned back, still keeping his bright eyes on me.

'Suppose I do some explaining? For a start, you don't know anything about the Mordifords, I suppose.'

'Nothing.'

'I'm not surprised. Totally undistinguished family, we are. But my grandfather started an export company to Australia at a time when practically the only other things being exported were convicts. By the time you get to my uncles and my mother, Australia was looking up and the company was doing very nicely. That's where the family

12

money comes from.'

Along with inscribed gold watches, holidays in the Alps and a strong and serviceable boot still gripped firmly in the glacier's jaws.

'There were three of them. My mother was the eldest but she blotted her copybook by running off and marrying a penniless teacher. Arthur was the elder brother, he was twenty-six when he died, and Gregory was three years younger. In the summer of 1880 they did what all the hearty young university men were doing at the time and went off to climb Mont Blanc. You saw the result.'

'What exactly happened?'

He shrugged.

'I can't give you any of the gory details. I only heard the story from my mother. Arthur and Gregory were climbing with a party and Arthur and one of the guides got swept down in an avalanche. I gather that sort of thing happens quite often.'

'Yes.'

'They never found Arthur's body. Uncle Gregory came back grief-stricken and never climbed again. He hates even talking about mountains. When I first went to work for him I made some casual mention of it and he wouldn't even reply.'

'Do you still work for your uncle?'

'Yes. He very decently paid for me to go to Oxford and when I came down he suggested I should join the family firm. His son Benedict was still at Harrow at the time and he needed somebody. I started at the bottom, more or less, and rose by my own efforts – also, more or less – to become company secretary. Uncle Gregory's come to depend on me quite a bit, which is how I come to be here.'

'Is his son with him, too?'

'Oh yes, Benedict's here, very much under protest. Then there's Beatrice, Gregory's daughter. As a matter of fact, Beatrice and I are engaged. It's unofficial for the moment because Gregory has this prejudice against cousins marrying, but I think Beatrice will be able to talk him round once this business is out of the way. All this is

13

very hard on Beatrice. It will be good for her to have another woman around.'

'I'm only here for a few more days, so I don't suppose I'll get a chance to meet her.'

I made no effort to sound polite.

'I'm sorry, I'm running ahead of myself, aren't I? Picture last Tuesday, if you would. Here are we, Uncle Gregory and I, at work in the office, when a telegram message arrives via the British Embassy in Paris. All very tactfully put, but the gist of it is that Uncle Arthur's turned up at last and what does Gregory want done with him? The poor chap nearly passed out.'

'So now you've all come here for the funeral?'

He sighed. 'Would that we had. Uncle Gregory's taken against mountains so badly that he can't bear to think of his brother being buried within sight of them. We've come out to collect him and take him home – which is where my troubles begin.'

'Bureaucracy?'

'French bureaucracy, which seems to be three times worse than any other kind. Also poor Uncle Gregory's got to view the remains and formally claim them. That's tomorrow. When I heard you'd already seen him I thought I'd scrape your acquaintance and if you turned out to be . . . well, not hysterical about the whole thing, find out what I could to prepare him.'

It seemed a reasonable objective to me. As factually as I could, I told him about the condition of the body, warning him about the missing lower leg and the caved-in ribs.

'You say his face is all right, though?'

'Surprisingly, apart from a deep gash in the forehead.'

'Would the ice do that?'

'It might, but it's more likely that it was his own ice-axe when the avalanche hit him. They even recovered the ice-axe.'

He was thoughtful, as if this detail brought the reality of what had happened closer.

'There's his watch, too, and his journal.'

'Journal? Where would that be now?'

'It went down with the body. They'll probably hand over his personal effects when your uncle goes to identify him. Part of the formalities.'

'Ah yes, those formalities. That's the other reason I wanted to speak to you.'

He shifted in his seat and pushed his coffee-cup aside, as if our meeting were now entering a new phase. I sensed, for all his casualness of manner, that there was a business agenda.

'Uncle and I are used to forms and officials and so on. It's the stuff of our business. The problem is, he hardly speaks a word of French and I don't know much that's any use. I mean, they dragged us through the usual stuff at school, but that's not much to the purpose when it comes to the coffin *de mon oncle*, so to speak.'

'I'm sure they'll be able to find you an interpreter.'

'Yes . . . The point is . . .'

He was twirling the coffee-spoon in his fingers, capable fingers on square hands.

'It struck me that it would make things easier for him if we had an interpreter who was one of our own kind, so to speak.'

I got ready a firm refusal. I was prepared to be moderately sympathetic towards Uncle Gregory, but not to the extent of spending the last few days of my holiday with officialdom.

'There seem to be quite a few people here who know you and somebody mentioned you were practically bilingual in French. It struck me that since you'd been in at the start, as it were, you might be prepared to help us out.'

I took a deep breath, trying to suppress annoyance.

'Naturally, we'd pay you. Would four pounds a day sound all right?'

I took a second deep breath and thought about it. I hope I'm not mercenary by nature. On the other hand, two or three days' work at four pounds a day would fund another week in Chamonix and possibly the Mont Blanc climb as well. Since I am by profession a freelance translator it was no shame to accept a reasonable offer.

15

'Four pounds a day would indeed be all right.' Then I had to add, 'Too much, in fact.'

'Please don't let that worry you. Uncle Gregory's by no means short of money and you'd be doing him a great kindness. Of course, he'll be paying for your meals and accommodation as well.'

'I have accommodation.'

'I was hoping you might move in with us while this is going on. I'm sure you'd get on with Beatrice and it really would help her. Benedict is . . .' He seemed to be struggling with family loyalty, then took a moderate plunge. 'Well, let's say Benedict may not be the most thoughtful of brothers for the poor girl, at least not in his present mood.'

In the end I agreed to move in with them, though I'd have preferred to keep some of the day to myself. I tried one last objection.

'After all, you know nothing about me.'

He smiled.

'You might be surprised.'

From his tone, he obviously hadn't been wasting his time on the Chamonix gossip round. If he knew my record and still wanted my help, fair enough.

Hector Tenby settled the bill, asked where I was staying and said he'd call for me first thing in the morning. He offered politely to escort me back to my pension but I told him I wanted to stroll round the town for a while. After he'd gone, with a cheerful wave, it struck me that he seemed to know more about me than I knew about the Mordifords. Still, I was committed. That evening, in celebration of forthcoming wealth, I ordered ham in my omelette and an extra glass of wine. I drank it in a solitary toast to Arthur Mordiford. It seemed ironic that his slide down Mont Blanc should provide the means for my ascent of it, but surely no mountaineer could object to that.

THREE

HECTOR TENBY WAS AT THE door of my pension at ten
o'clock next morning, more formally dressed in a black
suit and hat. By then, I'd met my friends at the station,
told them that I shouldn't be walking with them for a few
days and tried to find out if anybody knew more than I did
about the Mordifords. All I gathered was that three of
them had attended the English church on Sunday
morning: Gregory Mordiford, a blonde girl who was
assumed to be his daughter and another man who
sounded from the description to be Hector. There'd been
no sighting of the son, Benedict. The family had been
objects of interest because everybody had heard the story,
but my informants didn't know of anybody who'd actually
talked to them. Nor did they know where they were
staying – surprisingly in a town where the local paper
listed the names of newcomers to the big hotels. I had my
bag packed ready when Hector arrived.

'Is that all? I was going to call a horse cab.'

'I'm sure we can walk faster than one of those horses. It
can't be very far.'

'It isn't. If you really don't mind walking it's probably a
good thing. It gives me a chance to fill in the card a bit
before you meet the others.'

He insisted on carrying my bag. At this time of day the
serious walkers and climbers were already way up the
mountain and the streets were given over to fashionable
strollers and invalids in bath chairs. Outside the big hotels
strings of mules waited patiently as tourists and picnic
baskets were hoisted on.

17

'Seems a jolly sort of place. I should warn you, this establishment where we're staying may strike you as a surprising choice. It's Uncle Gregory's doing and I must admit it's rather by way of adding to my worries about him. In fact, it's precisely the last place in the whole town I'd have chosen for us.'

'Is it that uncomfortable?'

'It's comfortable enough. It's the memories that are the problem. You see it's where he and Arthur and the rest of them were staying that summer Arthur died.'

'And your uncle chose to go back there?'

'Imagine Gregory and myself in the office again. It's the day after we got the telegram about Arthur and we're all in confusion, making arrangements to get out here as soon as possible. Just as I'm thinking about a hotel, this other telegram arrives. It's in English, a bit stilted but quite intelligible as far as it goes. Madame Martin presents her condolences and her compliments and if Mr Mordiford is returning to Chamonix she insists that he and any of his family must come and stay with her. The clerk brings it to me, I read it and take it to Gregory and naturally I ask him who is this Madame Martin. Whereupon he turns as white as a sheet and gasps out that she's the widow of the guide.'

'The guide who was killed in the avalanche at the same time as Arthur?'

'Exactly. Apparently the whole party of them were lodging in the guide's house. I suppose there weren't as many hotels around then. Anyway, seeing how it affected Gregory I naturally assumed that we shouldn't be taking up her invitation. I suggested I should draft a civil refusal then go along to Cook's to see about the tickets and a hotel. But Gregory wasn't having any of that. I had to telegram back that we thanked her for her kind invitation and the four of us would be arriving in a couple of days.'

'What happened when you arrived?'

'Absolutely nothing on the face of it, except a very kind welcome. Rooms ready for us, and very pleasant rooms they are, superb food. No tactless talk about the old days.'

'Then why are you worried?'

'Uncle Gregory, mainly. He keeps looking at Madame as if she were some kind of bomb about to go off. Or *bombe au chocolat* perhaps, seeing as she's a confectioner. Anyway, he practically tiptoes round her.'

'One of these formidable French widows?'

'Anything but, to look at her. She's tiny and can't weigh much more than a hundred pounds. But she's quite the businesswoman. Look at this.'

He steered me gently towards a shop window that was a masterpiece of sweetmeats, sugared almonds spilling from shells, tiny fruit tarts like jewels arranged in rows, baskets of truffles ornamented with dried mountain flowers. Down the middle of the display marched a row of miniature chocolate Mont Blancs, with icing sugar for snow. You could even pick out the long streak of it that represented the Glacier des Bossons.

'Madame Martin makes those, the truffles and the little mountains. Probably makes a packet from them, judging by the prices they sell at.'

'I suppose that was her way of making a living after her husband was killed. Enterprising lady.'

I wondered if it was simply female efficiency that scared Gregory Mordiford.

'Then there's the son and daughter. I don't suppose they mean to make things worse, but they do.'

'The son's a mountain guide too, isn't he? I've met him.'

He glanced at me. We walked on.

'Yes. Luckily he's out guiding most of the day, but he's looming around in the evenings. Hardly ever says anything but "Good evening", but it's the presence, if you know what I mean.'

'Memories?'

'Yes. I suppose the man's got a right to look like his father, but it must make poor Gregory feel like Hamlet with the ghost sitting down to dinner with him, or am I thinking of whatshisname in Macbeth? Anyway, not comfortable.'

'And Madame Martin's daughter's a problem too?'

'Yes, though it's probably not her fault either.'

19

He sounded more doubtful about that.

'Only probably?'

He hesitated for a few steps, then:

'Oh well, you'd better know about it as you're coming to stay with us. Not that he isn't making it as obvious as a horse in a drawing-room in any case. It's Ben's attitude to her that's the problem.'

'Liking or disliking?'

'Liking, very much so. The fact is, Miss Bray, my cousin is flirting with Mademoiselle Martin quite outrageously.'

'With or without encouragement from her?'

I glanced at his face and was amused to see a struggle going on. Of course, a gentleman should not speak lightly of a woman's reputation, but then this woman was foreign and perhaps that made a difference.

'Well . . . I can't say she's been actively discouraging. In fact, she seems rather amused by it, flattered even. But she must be at least six years older than he is – after all, she can't be younger than thirty – so she's probably used to that kind of thing. She's a good-looking woman, no denying it.'

I told him that I didn't see the problem because it didn't sound as if a little flirting would do either of them any harm. Tactless in the circumstances possibly, but since Benedict wouldn't have known his Uncle Arthur he could hardly be expected to go into mourning.

'Not the point, I'm afraid. I'm sure Ben's doing it entirely to annoy his father and he's succeeding.'

'You say he came here under protest?'

'He says the whole thing's morbid and unnecessary. When he first heard about it he flatly refused to come with us, but Gregory's adopting a new policy of being firm with Ben and this is the first fruit of it.'

'What's your cousin's profession?'

'That's the problem. Ben thinks he's a painter. After Cambridge his father wanted him to take up his responsibilities in the family firm, but he insisted on going to the Slade. Gregory footed the bills on the assumption that Ben would get art out of his system and see reason.'

'Did he?'

'Not in Gregory's book. It looked quite hopeful earlier this year. He quarrelled with all his teachers at the Slade and told them they hadn't had a new idea since Ruskin. But then he went to Gregory and said the only place to study painting was Paris and he wanted to go there. That was when Gregory put his foot down and I'm afraid the battle's been going on ever since. Poor Beatrice tries to be the peace-maker but she'll break down if they go on like this. She's a very sensitive girl. She's published a volume of poetry, you know.'

I could imagine it, an affair with wide margins and parchment paper, paid for by a loving father. I told myself not to be prejudiced against the girl by a doting fiancé's description. In my experience people described as very sensitive are usually tough as saddle-leather and self-absorbed to the point of mania.

'Why doesn't Benedict simply take himself off to Paris? He's over twenty-one, I suppose? He doesn't need his father's permission.'

'No, but he does need his father's money. He hasn't even got enough of his own to starve in a garret. To be honest, I think he might be near the point of surrender. There've even been sightings of him in the office recently. If Gregory's lucky, this might be Ben's last little kicking fit before he settles down to work. But I must admit that I shall be glad when it's all over.'

We were walking up the street towards the church. Since he was so open about the family affairs I decided to raise a tactless question.

'Madame Martin has said nothing to you or your uncle about the accident?'

'Not a word that I know of.'

'I was wondering if your uncle's nervousness might be because he knows his brother was in some way to blame for her husband's death.'

He stopped dead, staring at me.

'Now why in the world should you think that?'

'No reason, except that avalanches are often triggered off by something and guides are careful people. It only

21

takes an inexperienced climber to do one thing wrong and the whole party's in trouble.'

He began walking again, but more slowly.

'You're saying that Uncle Arthur did something stupid?'

'Only that it's a possibility. He might have been a very good climber for all I know.'

'But how would Madame Martin know in any case? She wasn't there and they were both killed.'

'There'd be more than one guide in the party, so of course there'd be discussions about it after they came down.'

Hector was looking so thoughtful that I was sorry I'd raised the possibility.

'I'm probably quite wrong. If she really did blame Arthur surely she'd want to keep away from his family rather than inviting you to stay?'

'I hope so.'

But he said nothing else for the rest of the walk. We crossed in front of the church and turned to the right.

'That's the Maison Martin.'

It stood across a cobbled courtyard, a tall but cheerful-looking house painted in a warm cream colour with green shutters thrown back from the windows and a green painted bench by the door. Pigeons wheeled round the steep tiled roof, wings flashing in the sunshine, and scarlet geraniums frothed from intricately carved window-boxes on ground and first floors. As we came nearer another scent merged with geraniums, a rich waft of warm chocolate. Hector knocked on the door and after a little delay it was opened by a maid in a black dress and white apron. She smiled at Hector and showed us into the front parlour. It was a small sunny room, with pots and vases of mountain flowers on every horizontal surface. Then the door opened and in came Madame Marie Martin.

There are some people that strike you as a force of nature and she was one of them. As Hector had said she was small and had to tilt her head to look up at me, but she did it with a smile that made my height and her lack of it an ice-breaking joke between us. She was probably in her early sixties and her hair was white, but piled up like ice-cream with a little rondel of black and white lace on the top that was more decoration than widow's cap. Her dress was black and high-necked, made of fine silk that made a cool slithering sound when she moved, like snow sliding off branches. The face could have belonged to a woman twenty years younger, with smooth skin over high cheekbones and restless dark eyes. We touched hands and she began speaking at once, fast and in French. It was a little speech of welcome, how she hoped I would be comfortable there and how helpful it would be to Mr Mordiford to have me. But there was more to it than that. She knew I'd been hired as an interpreter and was very sensibly testing my ability. I replied in kind and was approved by a smile and a quick nod of her neat head.

Hector, who'd been listening in the uneasy way of somebody marooned on the wrong side of a river of talk, said he'd go and get the others. When he came back the small room seemed full of people.

'Miss Bray, may I introduce Miss Mordiford?'

I noticed he didn't introduce her as his fiancée, but then her father was standing only a few feet away. She was a sturdy girl and came at me, pulsing emotion. Her eyes were an intense blue that was almost violet, but misted over with tears recently shed or just held in check. She was dressed in swirls of lavender with fair hair coiled over her ears in a vaguely medieval style. Her hand was soft and yet it gripped mine for longer than needed in an introduction, like a swimmer being pulled out of a pool, and I noticed her fingernails were bitten to the quick. She seemed an odd mixture of desperation and calculation. Once she'd been introduced, her eyes went to Hector and stayed on him.

'My uncle, Gregory Mordiford.'

He was a prosperous-looking man, dapper to the point of being dandyish, even in black. He was in his fifties, clean shaven, his neatly cut hair sprinkled with grey. He had full lips like his nephew and unusually round brown eyes that gave him the wary, nocturnal look of a lemur. His hand-shake had a nervous twitch to it.

23

'Miss Bray, I can't tell you how grateful we are to you for coming to our rescue. Hector's told me you're breaking your holiday. It really is most kind of you.'

I was feeling guilty already about the four pounds a day. Hector said: 'And this is my cousin, Benedict Mordiford.'

I put out my hand. He bent and kissed it. I saw the look on his father's face and knew he was only doing it to annoy.

'Yes, how very kind of you to rescue us.'

There was no mistaking the sarcasm. I told myself that I'd allow him this one bite, but if he tried it again he'd get a kick. He was taller than the rest of the family and quite good-looking in a moody and self-conscious way. His dark hair was long and needed washing, his watchful eyes sunk deep into their sockets under black eyebrows that met in the middle. He wore white flannels and a creased white linen jacket in an obvious and deliberate contrast to his father's meticulous black.

Gregory and Hector were both carrying hats and gloves, ready to go. We'd agreed on the way that the unpleasant business of the morgue should be got over as soon as possible. Gregory glanced at his son.

'You'd better go up and change quickly, Ben. We don't want to keep Miss Bray waiting.'

Benedict lounged against a chair back.

'Oh, I don't think I'll bother after all, thank you very much.'

'Ben.'

It came in three different tones from the three members of his family: a sharp command from Gregory, a plea from Beatrice, the start of a reasoned case from Hector.

'You did say you would, you know, and your father is rather depending on it.'

'Oh, I'm sure he can depend on you, Hector. He usually does, doesn't he?'

Benedict glanced at me, probably checking the audience to make sure he was being offensive enough. Hector started to say something, then stopped himself. Beatrice put a hand on his arm then withdrew it hastily when she saw her father's face and put it on Benedict's instead.

24

'Poor Ben did have a headache this morning. I'm sure he . . .'

He shook off his sister's hand.

'My head is quite all right now, thank you, Beatrice. At any rate, it's clear enough to see no pleasure or profit in inspecting the mangled remains of a relative in whom I should almost certainly have had no interest, even if I had ever met him.'

On that line he tried to stroll casually from the room, but found his father blocking his path.

'Benedict, I've had as much as I can stand from you. You are coming with us whether you like it or not.'

He stared down at his father and managed an ironic grin. Beatrice was crying. Hector had on a stern expression that indicated his cousin should expect no support from him. Benedict looked round, grinned at me and shrugged.

'If you insist, Father, but you'll have to take me as I am. My widow's weeds are at the cleaners.'

This might have been a shot at Madame Martin, the only person in the room he hadn't managed to offend in the last few minutes. The upshot of his attempted rebellion was that he climbed into the horse cab with his father, Hector and me looking like a refugee from a village cricket team with low sartorial standards.

The morgue was on the outskirts of town and little was said on the journey there. We found officials waiting for us, efficient but tactful, and a hovering curate from the English church. Gregory went in first to see the body on his own while the rest of us waited in a bleak little room with a strong disinfectant smell that reminded me of Holloway Prison. I was sitting next to Hector.

'You warned him?'

'About the missing leg and so on? Yes. It's only a formal identification, after all. He doesn't need to do more than glance.'

Benedict ignored us, hunched in a chair over a book that he'd fished out of his pocket as soon as he sat down. When Gregory came back five minutes or so later he

looked like a man making a determined effort not to be sick.
Hector took his arm and murmured that it was all right, it
was over now, the English curate added soothing noises and
the officials produced brandy. Benedict didn't look up
from his book. One of the officials asked a question and I
translated it for Hector.

'Do any of the rest of you want to see him?'

'Oh lord, I'd better, I suppose. What about you, Ben?'

Benedict shook his head without looking up. By the time
Hector came back, Gregory had recovered enough to sign a
paper formally identifying the corpse of his brother,
Arthur Mordiford.

One of the officials produced a brown paper parcel and
unwrapped it on the table.

'His watch, monsieur, his ice-axe and that felt object is his
hat. Perhaps you'd be kind enough to sign for them.'

Gregory gave a little shudder when he looked at the
broken ice-axe, but signed without comment. The parcel
was done up again and Hector took custody of it. There was
still the lengthy business of the transport of the body to
England to be arranged and the officials were in favour of
going back to the mayor's office and beginning it at once.
But Hector decided that his uncle needed time to recover
and Gregory didn't take much persuading. On the way back
in the pony cab he closed his eyes and put a hand to his
chest.

'Do you feel ill?'

His brown eyes looked into mine, full of pain.

'Please don't worry. It's no more than nervous indigestion. I'm afraid I'm subject to it even at the best of times.'

All the way back he was trying to hide delicate little burps
and when we arrived he decided to take a glass of hot water
up to his room and lie down. Benedict had already
disappeared. Hector stood in the hall, still holding the
parcel.

'I'm afraid that's it for today. By the time uncle's
recovered the bureaucrats will have shut up shop.'

'I'll go along to the mayor's office and make an appointment for tomorrow morning, if you like.'

'Would you? I suppose I'd better find somewhere to put this. I can understand the watch, but what are we supposed to do with his hat and his confounded ice-axe?'

'I don't think your uncle will want it.'

'No. I think it was that great trough in his forehead that really got to poor Gregory. It's pretty bad, isn't it? I suppose he'd be unconscious or dead already when it happened, but still . . .'

His voice trailed away, but he seemed reluctant to move.

'Didn't you tell me they found his journal with him? There's no book with this lot.'

'It might be at the mayor's office. I'll remember to ask them about that tomorrow.'

My room was in the attic, a comfortable cabin of polished pinewood and clean white linen. I unpacked my bag then went to the mayor's office to make the appointment as promised. It was a good excuse to avoid lunch with the Mordiford family, in the hope that the row would have blown through before we all met in the evening. With the same idea in mind I spent most of the afternoon around the town and didn't get back to the Maison Martin until it was time for dinner. After the maid had let me in I lingered in the long hallway, looking at the photographs of mountains and mountaineers along the wall. Some of them dated from an earlier generation, and one, larger than the rest, was in the place of honour by the bottom of the stairs.

There were six men on it, staring out with the strained and heroic expressions that come from having to stand still for a long time in front of a plate camera. The two on the outside were guides with coils of ropes on their shoulders, one tall and thin, the other small and Italian-looking. The four in between were their clients in thick tweed suits, beards and new felt hats. It was a good photograph. You could tell that their suits were of the best quality, their boots properly nailed and dubbined. One of them had his jacket open and you could see the watch-chain neatly looped across his waistcoat. I'd seen the watch it led to. I knew the inscription on it. I was sure of that even before I saw the date at the lower right hand corner of the picture mount: July 1880. If you looked hard at the figure left of centre you could recognise Gregory's round eyes.

I stood staring at it for a long time. When I heard a man's footsteps coming down the stairs I assumed, without glancing up, that it was Hector.

'I think this must be the Mordiford party.'

No answer. I glanced up and saw a pair of legs in climbing breeches and long woollen stockings.

'Yes, that is their party.'

Pierre Martin spoke carefully, in his heavily accented English. He came down and stood beside me, looking at the photograph.

'Is that your father?'

I pointed to the tall, thin guide. He nodded, but I'd hardly needed to ask. The likeness was clear enough to explain why Gregory found his presence disturbing. We stared at it without saying anything. Guides and clients on a summer day almost half a lifetime away, healthy and pleased with themselves and the Glacier des Bossons waiting. It was hard to look at the photograph without wanting, over the years, to shout a warning to them. I wondered if Pierre Martin felt like that as he passed the photograph every day on his way to work. He'd get used to it, probably. And yet I sensed from the way he was looking at it that he'd never quite got used to it, that it still worried him in some way. Before I could decide whether to break the silence a door opened along the passage, there was a whiff of herbs and casserole and Madame Martin's voice calling to him. He apologised and went, leaving me still looking at the picture. A nice touch, the way the four of them were leaning so confidently on their ice-axes. Poor Gregory.

FOUR

GREGORY SEEMED BETTER AT DINNER, although still red about the nose. It was a formal meal, four courses served by two maids, with Madame Martin presiding at the head of the table. Pierre Martin, who'd changed out of his guide's clothes into an ordinary suit, sat at the far end with an empty place beside him. Once I saw Madame Martin glance at it, catch her son's eye and give a little shrug. Conversation was determinedly in English, on neutral subjects like the coming of the railway and the numbers of tourists. Benedict said nothing, ate little and concentrated on emptying his wine glass and catching the eye of one of the maids to have it filled again. We avoided any mention of what had brought the Mordifords to Chamonix until Beatrice suddenly plunged us into it. Up to that point, she'd contributed almost as little as her brother. Her intense blue eyes concentrated on Madame Martin who'd just been talking about her plans to convert two more rooms into accommodation for visitors.

'What room did Uncle Arthur's fiancée stay in?'

Her voice, not loud but very clear, fell into the conversation like a silver spoon dropped on a stone floor. All her family stared at her, Gregory looking reproachful, and even Marie Martin seemed surprised.

'She never stayed with us. We didn't have enough room, so she and her mother stayed in the house next door.'

'Did Uncle Arthur have a fiancée? How very tragic.'

Benedict didn't sound as if he thought it tragic at all. His sister turned on him.

'Well, it was. Can you imagine what it must have been

29

like for the poor girl, waving him off in the morning and never seeing him again? No wonder she went mad.'

'Who told you that?'

Gregory's voice was sharp. Beatrice glanced at Hector, appealing for his help.

'I did, as a matter of fact, Uncle. My mother mentioned something about it. According to her, the name was Daisy Belford. She wouldn't accept that Arthur was dead and kept wandering round among the glaciers looking for him.'

'A kind of goat-girl Ophelia. Very picturesque, it must have been. D'you suppose she twined edelweiss in her hair?'

Beatrice gave Benedict the kind of sisterly look that would raise blisters on a skin not hardened against it and turned to her father.

'Is it true?'

'A little exaggerated, I think.'

He looked miserable. Hector had been right in saying that he hated talking about it, and yet Hector was looking at Beatrice with approval. Dragging grief-stricken fiancées to the dinner table might be her way of reminding her father that she considered herself engaged to her cousin. She persisted.

'But there was a fiancée called Daisy Belford?'

He nodded.

'And she came here with him and went mad after he was killed?'

'As far as I can remember she was always a little unstable. I never knew her well. This must all be very tedious for Madame Martin and Miss Bray and I think we've discussed it quite enough.'

No further mention was made of Arthur Mordiford until the dessert stage – delicious little bilberry tartlets in almond-flavoured pastry. Gregory looked at them longingly, took a drink of wine then said to me: 'Did the mayor's office know anything about the journal?'

The change in the atmosphere was immediate. A chair creaked. I explained that I'd only seen a clerk to make an appointment and would ask about the journal tomorrow. There was an awkward silence, broken by Madame Martin.

'Do you mean the book found with Mr Mordiford? That did not go to the mayor's office. We kept it here for you.'

Quiet sensation round the table. Gregory looked alarmed, Hector surprised and even Benedict took an interest.

'How did it come to be . . . ?'

Gregory stopped in mid-question and changed tack.

'I should be very interested to see it. I don't suppose it will still be readable, but even so . . .'

I was on the point of assuring him that it was still quite readable but stopped myself. If I told him I'd read some of it that would take us straight back to the discovery of the body in the glacier and the less he dwelt on that the better. I glanced towards Pierre and his eyes met mine, level and direct. He was warning me about something, I was sure of that, but didn't know what. As clearly as if he were guiding me over a tricky piece of climbing that look told me to step carefully. When in doubt, trust the guide. I said nothing.

Madame Martin stood up.

'If you will all excuse me, I will go and fetch it now.'

There was silence when she'd gone, except Benedict whispered something to Beatrice and she looked annoyed. Gregory kept his eyes down and poured himself more wine. I guessed that now he was close to touching the book he was nervous about his reaction to it. I wished for his sake that Madame Martin had contrived a less public way of handing it over. She was back in a few minutes, empty handed.

'I regret very much that it is not available this evening. Our maid who cleans the rooms has accidentally taken my bureau key home with her, so it is locked up. She'll be back early in the morning and I will bring the book to you at breakfast.'

I didn't know if Gregory believed this, but I certainly didn't. Madame Martin ran an orderly household, not the kind where cleaning maids would be permitted to get their

31

hands on keys to private bureaux, let alone walk off with them. I glanced at Pierre again but his eyes were on his mother. I was certain he believed this nonsense about the maid no more than I did. When the front door opened and closed and feet came running lightly up the stairs Marie Martin seized on it as a diversion.

'Sylvie, just as we're finishing.'

Then the dining-room door opened and all the light in the room shifted to the woman who entered. Some women have this effect, perfectly likeable women as well as some totally infuriating ones. It's not simply a matter of beauty, more of a vitality that seems more highly charged than normal so that you watch them to see what's going to happen next. Sylvie Martin wasn't as young as she looked at first glance but she seemed as fresh as mountain air. Her eyes were huge and dark in a small face, her hair a deep chestnut colour and piled casually, with little tendrils hanging down to emphasise a slim neck. She wore a cluster of fresh marguerites in the band of her straw hat and a bunch of yellow bell-shaped flowers tucked into the belt of her blue skirt. The bottom of her skirt was white with dust, her small shoes scuffed from walking. Benedict was sitting opposite the door and when she came in I saw him smile for the first time. He was on his feet before the other men could react. Beatrice noticed that too and I could see it didn't please her. Sylvie Martin smiled at us all and began an apology in French for her lateness. She'd been visiting friends up at Argentière, missed the train back and had to wait for a lift on a hay cart.

'Tell her I hope the hay was soft.'

As Benedict hadn't taken his eyes off Sylvie, it took a while to realise that the command was directed at me. I passed the remark on to her in French, omitting the suggestiveness he'd managed to put into the original. From the smile she gave him I think the message got there anyway.

'Ask her if she'll give me one of her pretty flowers.'

His eyes were on the bunch at her slim waist. Gregory snapped at him: 'Miss Bray isn't here to interpret your poor jokes and I'm sure Mademoiselle Martin has better things to do than to listen to them.'

Again, the message got there in spite of the language difficulties. She touched the yellow flowers and smiled at him again.

'Yellow gentian.'

Her voice was low and musical. Another, higher voice snapped across it.

'Gentian lutea.'

Beatrice Mordiford used the Latin name like a riding switch. She added, for good measure, 'It's really quite common in the Alps.'

The way she looked at Sylvie showed she thought there were other things in the Alps equally common. Although Sylvie probably didn't understand the words, she couldn't have missed the look but she only gave a little smile and turned away.

'My daughter's very interested in botany, aren't you, Beatrice?'

Gregory's embarrassed remark to me might have been meant as an apology but it didn't help the atmosphere, leaving Madame Martin to step more smoothly into the breach.

'We make a drink from the roots of the yellow gentian. It's good for the digestion.'

It struck me that she was also seizing a chance to escape from the awkward business of the journal with what I was coming to recognise as her usual efficiency. Gregory had never heard of Gentian as a drink, so the maid who'd just brought in the coffee was sent to fetch a bottle of it and a tray of liqueur glasses. It was a colourless liquid in a wine bottle with a handwritten label showing the previous year's date. I asked Madame Martin if she made it herself.

'Yes. It's an old recipe passed down in my husband's family.'

I was familiar with Gentian so sipped cautiously. It has a bitter taste with an earthy tang to it that you could take as the flavour of the gentian roots themselves, reaching deep for their life into mountain soil. I watched the others with amusement. Beatrice took one sniff at her glass, made a face and pushed it away untasted. Hector drank his at a gulp and looked as if he wished he hadn't. Benedict sipped, shook his head and went back to his wine, raising his glass towards Sylvie. Only Gregory drank as if he enjoyed it and accepted a second glass on the grounds that it would cure his indigestion. Soon after that the party broke up. Madame Martin wished us good evening and went downstairs, with Sylvie and Pierre following. Benedict disappeared soon afterwards and Beatrice announced that she and Hector were going out for a stroll. Gregory didn't look very happy about that, but said nothing, except that he thought he'd have an early night. He looked tired and it was clear that his experience of the morgue was still weighing him down. I went out for a stroll myself, being careful not to intrude on Beatrice and Hector, got back as the light was going and went straight up to my room.

I didn't see the book at first. The electricity that lit the main rooms of the Maison Martin stopped short before it got to my attic so I had to light the lamp on the bedside table. As its glow spread round the little room I sat on the bed, looking forward to the time when the Mordifords' affair would be finished and I could go climbing again. Then I realised that there was something on the table that hadn't been there when I went out. I didn't want to touch it at first but after thinking about it I unwrapped the covering carefully and took out a small book with a stained blue cover. On the title page, in strongly-looped copperplate handwriting, were the words: *Chamonix. Summer 1880*. Underlined. Then a list of five names: *Arthur Mordiford, Gregory Mordiford, Thomas Mercer, Edward Dean*. There was a space before the fifth name: *Lucien Martin, chief guide*.

I laid it down on the quilt and stared at it. I had no doubt it was the book I'd seen picked out of the Glacier des Bossons, near Arthur's body. The book that was supposed to be locked up in Marie Martin's private bureau, with the key in her cleaning maid's pocket. The question was, who had put it there for me to find and why? The list of suspects almost certainly narrowed down to two, but that left the other question unanswered. The only way to answer it was to do what somebody obviously intended me to do and read the journal. I read.

Tuesday. A day of preparations. On the earnest recommendation of M. Martin we presented our compliments to the village grocer and appointed him our provisioner. We placed an initial order for two locally cured hams, two boxes of plain biscuits, five pounds of cheese, two jars of Carlsbad plums, two dozen bottles of claret and, on the insistence of our guide, several pounds of dried sausage as eaten by the local herdsmen. Much debate in our party as to whether mule or goat main constituent of said sausages. Bought two coils of rope and an ice-axe for myself. Arranged that we should walk up as far as the Plan de l'Aiguille tomorrow, to accustom ourselves to the altitude.

I turned the page, moved the lamp closer and followed the progress of that modest first day's walk. They'd got up to the Plan de l'Aiguille, well below the summer snowline, in company with two guides, four porters, six of the bottles of claret, one jar of plums, a ham and some of the sausage. The party also included 'the guide's sagacious dog and his young son to help carry the ropes'. It struck me that this boy might be Pierre. As far as I'd seen, there was only one son in the Martin household. He'd have been no more than a child thirty years ago, around ten years old perhaps, but a guide's son would begin to learn his trade early. I felt, unreasonably, annoyed with the Mordiford party for their patronising tone, so sure that the world and its inhabitants were created for the amusement of young Englishmen on holiday. But they were no worse than the rest of their kind. They seemed even to have accepted their guide's advice in using the first two weeks of their holiday to improve their fitness and mountaineering skills before the attempt on Mont Blanc. The writer had kept his journal conscientiously day by day, each day on its own double page. Some entries were illustrated with lively but unskilful sketches of chamois, marmottes and rock formations.

Towards the end of their first week they went on a cart up the valley to Argentière and started out up the glacier there, but it was too late in the day to do any serious climbing. *Lucien annoyed with us for starting too late. Took the opportunity on the glacier to show me how to use my new ice-axe to stop myself sliding. Good sport once you learn the trick of it.* It was on this day that he marked the first star in his journal, a little asterisk inked in beside the date, like the signs they put in the Baedeker guides for a good ruin or unmissable view. After that I was looking out for more stars as I read, wondering what made particular days stand out. A two-day climb on the Aiguilles Rouges, sleeping out in a herdsman's hut, rated two stars, which was understandable. In the first ten days there were three one-star days, then this two-star. A good holiday so far.

Then the puzzle. Their eleventh day was one of those disappointments you get in mountain country, even in summer. The day started misty but, in spite of their guide's warning that the weather would get worse, they insisted on setting out.

Mist thicker as we climbed, turning first to fine drizzle then to downpour. By our midday halt, as soaked as spaniels, it was decided that we should retreat to Chamonix. Ted dropped full brandy bottle on way down and broke it. No birds, no views.

A miserable day altogether and yet beside the date he'd put three stars. Was he being sarcastic? Apparently not, because next day the same rating was given to a light-hearted picnic near the source of the River Arve at the Col de Balme when the weather had improved. *Tom attempted to bathe in mountain stream, but abandoned the experiment owing to cold. Tried to converse with two mountain maidens herding goats but they fled laughing, taking goats with them. Comfortable journey down valley, somewhat hilarious, in cart full of straw along with rooster in cage.*

36

I stared at the asterisks then started laughing. I'd have guessed earlier if it weren't for our habit of thinking that our parents' generation were made of cooler flesh and blood than ourselves. Daisy Belford, the fiancée, lodged in the house next door. She was chaperoned by her mother, but mothers can't be everywhere. A kiss at least, or two or three. Not for me to speculate further about what had been revealed so oddly. But I wondered if the days had seemed long to her, sitting embroidering in the shade or perhaps taking decorous little trips on mule-back while the men were walking up glaciers and plunging naked into mountain streams. Then down the men would come in the evening and Daisy would jump up from her embroidery to welcome Arthur, bronzed and pleased with himself among his friends. I was glad if those asterisks meant she'd found some excitement in the holiday too, then I remembered Beatrice's story of how it had ended for her, the icy Ophelia wandering mad among the glaciers.

The men's picnic seemed to be a day of relaxation before the serious business of the attempt on Mont Blanc. They hired three more guides in addition to Lucien Martin, one for each of them, plus nine porters. Reading between the lines it struck me that Lucien Martin was far from confident about the ability of his messieurs and was planning their ascent in very easy stages. They were to spend their first night camped out on the familiar Plan de l'Aiguille, getting up early the following morning to begin the crossing of the glaciers. They'd left the Maison Martin on the morning of 25 July 1880, which was probably when the picture in the hall was taken. The journal for the first day was written at the camp on the Plan de l'Aiguille in a hand less neat than usual. I imagined him sitting outside a tent, balancing his journal on his knees. It began with the passage I'd read already:

We are camped here on a stony meadow, with the town spread out below us and the glaciers and the great peaks above. Our expedition at rest has the air of a picnic party. One of the guides, Antoine, is preparing our evening meal of soup, cold

*fowl, ham and asparagus. Tom has insisted on celebrating
the start of our venture by breaking out two of the six bottles
of champagne reserved for our arrival at the summit. We
made an impressive party as we left our lodgings this
morning and children and idlers came out to watch. Our
order of march was M. Martin and we four, then the other
guides, then the porters, finally M. Martin's son with the dog
and a spare rope. We are assured that the dog will go back
with a porter from our present camping place, but the lad
may be allowed to go with us as far as the hut at the Grands
Mulets rocks.*

Unusually, he spread over to a second double page to set
out their plans for the following day.

*Lucien Martin is eloquent about the difficulties as usual and
seems concerned that we are taking this attempt too lightly.
He tells us that an early start is essential because of the
danger of being hit by rock-falls down the couloirs of the
Aiguille du Midi as the sun melts the ice. Once we begin
crossing the Glacier des Bossons we must look out for
crevasses, follow our guides exactly – but exactly, messieurs
– and stop when they tell us. By lunchtime we should have
reached the refuge hut on the first of the Grands Mulets rocks
in the middle of the glacier. Having heard that the refuge is
small and uncomfortable we suggested that, if conditions are
good, we might press on to the summit the same day. Lucien
will have none of this. Much talk of crevasses, avalanches
and seracs crashing down in the warmth of the afternoon
sun. So we are to pass at least one night in a hut clinging like
a barnacle to the rock, possibly even a second night on our
way down.*

*With all this talk of perils and exertions we were doubtful
about the proposition that our guide's son, Pierre, should be
allowed to go with us to the Grands Mulets. We might have
refused, but he came to ask our permission in an English
speech so carefully rehearsed that we had not the heart.
Antoine is shouting that the soup is ready, and after our meal
we must go early to bed. I look forward as eagerly as the rest*

*of them to standing on the summit the day after tomorrow
and yet I must confess that some of my thoughts tonight stray
to a certain room in a certain house down in the valley.
When I look down at the lights of the town below us as
darkness falls I shall almost persuade myself that I can pick
out the light of one particular lamp.*

A rare burst of emotion from the young Mordiford. It
looked as if my guess had been right. I paused before
turning the page, reluctant to go on to the disaster I knew
was waiting for them. The next day's account should be of
their journey across the heavily crevassed glacier up to the
refuge at the Grands Mulets. If they started early he
should arrive there with plenty of time to write up his
journal before dark. I turned the page and found I was
looking at a blank, just two empty gaping pages. It hit me
with a sense of loss. I'd been expecting another day in their
company and being deprived of it somehow made Arthur
Mordiford's death more real than when I was looking
down at his body on the glacier. He must have been too
tired on that last evening to write up his journal, or
perhaps too shaken by the journey.

I must have moved the book closer to the lamp because I
saw that although the page I was looking at was blank,
there was writing on the next. I turned the page and
couldn't believe what I was seeing. There were just a few
words written in firmly pencilled black capitals: *THE
WOMAN'S A WHORE AND THERE'S AN END ON'T.*

FIVE

I FELT MY HAND DRAWING away from the book as if I'd
come across a scorpion in a rock garden. I recognised the
quotation. It was Dr Samuel Johnson at his worst, talking
about a woman with a persistently unfaithful husband
who'd taken a lover of her own at last. But what on earth
was it doing in a climber's journal? There was no way of
telling from the block capitals whether it was in the same
hand as the rest, although there was a scholarly neatness
about them. A clear assumption was that it must have been
written by one of the four English members of the party
since the reading of Chamonix guides and porters was
hardly likely to extend to Boswell's *Life of Samuel Johnson*.

Daisy Belford? It looked as if something had gone
wrong with the idyll and whatever it was had happened
only after the party had left Chamonix for its attempt on
Mont Blanc. In his last entry the writer had been waxing
lyrical about the lighted window in the valley. It followed
that, after the entry had been written, either the author
had learned something that totally changed his opinion or
one of the other three had got hold of his journal and
made his own bitter comment. That must have happened
at some time between dinner at the camp on the Plan de
l'Aiguille and whenever Arthur and the journal were
buried by the avalanche higher up the mountain. I
wondered if these emotional storms among the party
might have led to the carelessness that cost two lives.

What was more immediately worrying was that thirty
years later something was still going on. The journal
shouldn't be in my hands at all, but somebody, almost

certainly Pierre Martin or his mother, had gone to great trouble to make sure I read it before the Mordifords. Had they seen the whore quote and understood it? Were they simply trying to soften the blow for Arthur Mordiford's brother and, if so, what did they expect me to do about it? It was nearly midnight and I knew that I wouldn't sleep. I left the journal where it was, put on my hat and jacket and went down three flights of stairs quietly in stockinged feet, carrying my walking boots. No light came from under the doors I passed on my way down and I assumed that both the Martins and Mordifords were asleep. The front door was locked but there was a key on the inside of it. I let myself out and sat on the bench beside the door to put on my boots. The geraniums were still hoarding some of the warmth of the day and their scent hung in the air, but when I moved out of the shelter of the house there was a cool breeze coming off the summits with a whiff of snow to it. The moon was three-quarters full.

I walked past the church towards the path that eventually winds its way up to the Col du Brevent. The lower reaches are an easy stroll, even by moonlight, and I knew it well. I followed it as it slanted gently up through the pinewoods. The night was quiet, with only occasional scufflings from squirrels or owls, so it wasn't long before I knew I was being followed. If I stopped walking I could hear the soft fall of feet on pine needles, but the follower was keeping one turn of the track behind me and out of sight. I kept on at the same steady pace and came out on the edge of pastureland by a group of herdsmen's huts, silver grey and empty in the moonlight. Beyond them the path climbed more steeply across the pasture. If somebody wanted to follow me up there, he or she would have to come out of hiding. I walked on, counting to two hundred, and when I turned to look he was there, coming past the huts. He was walking as easily as a cat over a croquet lawn, face shadowed by his broad-brimmed hat. As I waited for him I turned and looked across the valley.

The snowy head of Mont Blanc was in front of me. Below it the Glacier des Bossons poured itself down with the moonlight turning its ice-blocks to abstract shapes of black and silver. Above the tumble of ice-blocks the Grand Mulets rocks reared up between two snowfields like sharks' fins splitting a calm sea. I didn't turn until I could hear him breathing.

'Good evening, Monsieur Martin.'

'Good evening, Miss Bray.'

He stopped a few steps below me, also looking towards the Grands Mulets, and for a few minutes neither of us said anything. In the end I broke the silence.

'I've been reading Mr Mordiford's journal.'

'Yes?'

He glanced at me and away again.

'Have you read it?'

'My English is not very good for reading.'

Hardly an answer.

'Has your mother read it?'

No reply at all to that, only a question delivered with such urgency that I knew it must be the reason for following me.

'Is there anything in it about what happened?'

'The accident? How could there be? He was killed.'

'Sometimes people have a kind of warning in their minds when something's going to happen.'

Even in his own language his words came slowly, as if he were trying them in his mind before speaking, like handholds he didn't trust.

'You mean did he have a premonition? No, there's nothing like that.'

He was close enough for me to feel the tension in him. There was something he needed desperately to know and he thought I might be in possession of it. I felt half-ashamed of myself for not being able to give it to him.

'You're in the journal. Apparently you made a little speech in English asking them to let you go with them as far as the Grands Mulets. Do you remember that?'

'A little.'

'You must have been very young.'

'I was twelve.'

'The journal ends with their camp on the first evening. He didn't write anything at the Grands Mulets. I don't know why. It shouldn't have been a long day, should it?'

'For a strong party, no, but they were not a strong party, and you know it is a dangerous area going up to the Grands Mulets, very crevassed.'

He was talking more easily now, like a professional. That day had been, among other things, his introduction to the family trade.

'We started late and I remember my father wasn't pleased about that. The conditions on the glacier were quite good and the weather was clear, but we had to go very slowly. My father and the other guides put ladders over some of the worst crevasses, but I remember one of the Englishmen was very nervous.'

'Arthur Mordiford or Gregory?'

'No, those two weren't so bad. It was one of the others. We had to let them rest a lot and I know my father was worried that we shouldn't reach the Grands Mulets refuge before sunset. We managed it, but the English messieurs were very tired.'

So none of them would have had the energy that night for writing bitter quotes in the journal.

'Was it a happy party? Did you have the impression that the Englishmen got on well together?'

'As far as I remember.'

How much would a twelve-year-old boy notice?

'What happened at the Grands Mulets hut?'

'Much as usual.'

'What's that?'

'We all ate. The Englishmen drank wine, and some of the porters too. We wrapped ourselves in blankets and tried to sleep.'

It must have been cramped in the hut, the four Englishmen, four guides, eight porters and the boy.

'Did your father say anything to you about his party?'

'He congratulated me because it was my first time up to the Grands Mulets but I wasn't as tired as they were. I asked him if he would let me go on to the summit with

43

them the next day, but he said I must wait in the refuge.'

'Did he seem worried about the next day?'

'A little worried perhaps, because they were not a strong party, but he could manage that.'

Below us the church clock struck one. I let the silence draw out. You couldn't see the hut on the Grands Mulets rocks from where we were standing, but there'd be climbers sleeping up there tonight between the moonlit snowfields.

'Did they get to the summit before the avalanche?'

'No, it happened very early the next morning.'

'Isn't that unusual? I thought it was usually after the sun got to the snow?'

'Avalanches don't always obey the rules.'

'What happened?'

'One of the other guides woke me. He asked me when my father had gone out. My father and Arthur Mordiford weren't in the hut.'

'How long had they been gone?'

'I don't know. The other guide was worried because it was light already and he knew my father wanted to start while it was still dark.'

'Surely somebody must have noticed when they went out.'

For some reason that made him uneasy and it was a while before he replied.

'People were going in and out of the hut most of the night.'

I could almost feel his face going red and couldn't help laughing.

'Of course. It would be cold up there and they'd been drinking. Serves them right for taking half a wine cellar up a mountain.'

He laughed too, with a touch of embarrassment.

'So there were people coming and going all night and you wouldn't know who'd gone out when. What did you do?'

'The other guide, Antoine, and I went outside. It was quite light. They were both of them on the snow slope

44

below the rock. My father was closer to us. Then the snow started sliding. We shouted to them and my father tried to get out of the way, but he couldn't. The side of the avalanche caught him and carried him a long way down the slope. The rest of it poured down a crevasse. Mr Mordiford was in the way and he went into a crevasse with it.'

His voice was calm but when his arm accidentally brushed mine I could feel it shaking through his jacket.

'I'm sorry.'

'It doesn't matter.'

We began to walk back down the path, side by side.

'Has Mr Mordiford seen his brother's body at the morgue?'

'Yes.'

'What happened?'

'He was shaken – as you'd expect.'

I knew that he'd followed me with a question that still hadn't been answered. I'd have tried to answer it if I could, but I didn't know what it was. I did what I could to help him.

'Was Arthur Mordiford being careless, do you think?'

'In what way?'

'He should never have been down on the snowfield on his own, should he? Do you think he'd wandered off for some reason and your father had gone to look for him?'

'It's possible.'

No help there.

'This must be a strain for your mother, bringing back memories.'

'Of course.'

'It was kind of your mother to invite the Mordiford family to stay with you, but do you think it was wise?'

An impertinent question, but I had to get through to him somehow. He stopped and looked at me, as if considering whether to answer, then: 'No. I'm sure it was not wise, not wise at all.'

Simple puzzlement in his voice. Marie Martin had her own motives, but her son didn't know what they were. Surely he hadn't expected me to guess.

We walked on and came within sight of the church and

45

the town below it. All the houses were shuttered, not a light showing. I tried the direct approach.

'Why are you interested in the journal?'

I counted the steps, ten of them, before he spoke.

'My father was Mr Mordiford's guide. You know, it is a special relationship between a guide and his monsieur. The guide must do everything he can to keep his monsieur safe, even die if necessary.'

He stopped speaking, as if there was no more to be said.

'But your father was trying to do that, wasn't he? And he did die.'

'So did his monsieur.'

'And that still matters to you, after all this time?'

He didn't answer.

'You want to know that your father did everything he could to keep him alive, is that it?'

He nodded.

'I think you should set your mind at rest on that. You can tell from your journal that your father was a very good guide, very conscientious. If what happened was anybody's fault, I'm sure it was Arthur Mordiford's, not his.'

He walked with head bowed, not answering, and I decided to leave it at that. When we got to the house he thanked me and said that he would go in by a side door and I should use the front door. If the idea was to protect my reputation we'd left it rather late for that because as I went to the door I noticed a curtain twitching in a window on the second floor, where the guest rooms were. There was no way of telling whose room it was.

SIX

THE JOURNAL DISAPPEARED FROM MY room next morning as mysteriously as it had arrived. I left it on the bedside table when I went down to breakfast. Half an hour later I saw it again in the hands of Madame Martin. She carried it in with some ceremony as the Mordifords and I were sitting over our second cups of coffee. Gregory got up and took it awkwardly. I could see from Hector's expression that he feared another emotional crisis. If he'd known about the whore quote he'd have had even more cause for worry. I wondered if I should find some way of warning him, but I could hardly do that without betraying the strange behaviour of the Martins over the book.

'Shall I take it upstairs for you, Uncle?'

Gregory shook his head and went upstairs. At least he wouldn't have a chance to read the book straight away because we were due at the mayor's office in half an hour. When he came down five minutes later he was carrying hat and walking cane and the three of us went to begin the formalities of transporting a body across France.

It didn't help when we found that Gregory needed his passport to prove his own identity and it had been left back at the Maison Martin. Hector went to get it, but it took him some time so when the office closed for lunch we were nowhere near the end of the form-filling. Gregory managed well, but he seemed tired and preoccupied as we walked back. Hector glanced at me and raised his eyebrows.

'You know, Uncle, you could still cut this thing short if you wanted to. We could bury him here. You'd only have

47

to say the word and I'm sure the vicar could deal with it.'

I agreed, although I didn't say so. The graveyard of the English church was already the resting place of quite a few unfortunate climbers. But Gregory simply shook his head and took a tighter grip on his walking cane.

When we got back he went straight up to his room. Hector got me to ask the maid if Beatrice had gone out.

'No, Mademoiselle is in the courtyard. The boy brought some flowers for her.'

When I translated this to Hector it made more sense to him than it did to me.

'She asked Madame Martin to find a boy to go flower-hunting for her. She wants some Alpines for her pressed flower collection but she can hardly go off botanising herself in the circumstances.'

We walked along the narrow passageway past the chocolate-smelling kitchen to a courtyard at the back of the house. It was a sunny paved area with more geraniums and terracotta pots of herbs. Beatrice was enthroned at a round cast-iron table with a respectful lad standing at her shoulder, doling out plants carefully wrapped in sphagnum moss from a leather satchel. In a corner of the courtyard Sylvie, wearing fresh white, sprinkled some of the herb pots from a small watering can. It takes talent of a kind to water a pot of fennel ironically but she managed it, making it a comment on Beatrice's dogged botany. Ben lounged against the wall of the house, watching her and grinning. Beatrice was ignoring them both but when she saw Hector a great smile came over her face. Safe in her father's absence, he bent and kissed her on the forehead.

'How's Father?'

'Bearing up. What have you got there?'

She spread them across the table for him, gentians, campanulas, little feathery artemisias, while the boy stood beside her, bewildered by the interest in things that were commonplace to him. Hector bent over them, his hand gently on her shoulder.

'Any of the orchids you wanted?'

'I don't know yet. He doesn't know the scientific names

and I don't know them in French.'

I asked the boy about the orchids. He nodded vigorously and produced from his satchel a specimen wrapped with particular care. Beatrice seized it, unrolled it and gasped.

'*Cypripedium calceolus*. Good. They're really quite rare.'

It was the oddest of flowers with a kind of swollen yellow lip and maroon-coloured outer petals. His sister's gasp of excitement brought Ben languidly across to look at it.

'Ye gods, what's that?'

Before Beatrice could get her breath to tell him in Latin, Sylvie's amused voice cut in from behind him.

'*Sabot de Vénus*.'

'Venus's sabot?'

Sylvie laughed, drew her stockinged foot out of her shoe and curved it extravagantly, high-arched like a dancer's. It mimicked so perfectly the curve of the flower that Beatrice's hands went protectively to her specimen as if Sylvie intended it some mischief.

'Yes,' said Ben. 'Yes, I see.'

His eyes were on Sylvie's instep. She blushed a little and wiggled her foot back into her shoe, but stayed there behind Ben, close to the table.

Beatrice unwrapped her final specimens with annoyance in every gesture and Hector gave his cousin a look that told him to keep quiet. The last one was a tall pale yellow flower with feathery foliage. Beatrice frowned over it for a while and checked her Alpine flora before pronouncing it to be *Aconitum vulparia*.

'*Tue-loup*,' said Sylvie, from over Ben's shoulder.

I translated: 'Wolf-killer.'

'Why "wolf-killer"?'

'She says it's very poisonous. In the old days they used it to kill wolves and foxes.'

Without making any sign that she'd heard, Beatrice put her flowers into a cardboard box and took money from Hector to pay the boy. Ben and Sylvie drifted back to their corner and were laughing at something when Gregory appeared from the house, looking strained and minus his hat and walking cane. When he saw the two of them together the strain flashed into open annoyance.

'Ben, did you check the poste restante for me?'

'Sorry, Governor, I haven't got round to it yet and they'll have closed for lunch now. I'll get round there as soon as . . .'

'For goodness' sake, it's not much to ask, is it? Hector and I are doing everything else.'

Sylvie, wisely, had disappeared back into the house with her watering can. Beatrice and Hector, burdened with the box of flowers, followed Gregory back inside. I was on the point of going with them but Ben intercepted me.

'I wonder if you'd apply your linguistic skills to this, Miss Bray.'

He took a page of folded typescript out of his pocket and gave it to me. I scanned it, expecting some kind of joke or incivility.

'It's just a property agent's advertisement, for a shop in Geneva.'

'Yes, but what exactly does it say?'

Puzzled, I translated aloud for him. It was a description of a small boutique in a prime position close to Lake Geneva with the price correspondingly high. When I'd finished it he looked a little ill at ease and decided I was owed some kind of explanation.

'Mademoiselle Martin thinks it's an excellent business proposition. They'd run it as a combined chocolate and florist shop.'

'They're thinking of setting up shop in Geneva?'

'Yes, but as far as I can gather it's a matter of trying to raise the purchase price. Madame and Sylvie were talking about it while you were out. If they could find an investor to share . . .'

'Ben. Ben, where are you?'

Gregory's voice from inside, raised to a point just short of a bellow. Ben grimaced, gave me a mocking bow and sauntered inside, taking the property advertisement with him.

At lunch, family storm-clouds were hanging over the table again but we got as far as the peaches and pears before they broke. We were on our own, with none of the Martin family present.

'Ben, the proper place for reading is in the drawing-room, not at the table.'

Gregory's voice was as sharp as to a child. Ben looked up slowly, as if unsure that his father had been speaking to him.

'Oh, sorry, Father, I'm trying to improve my French. Could be a business asset, don't you think?'

'There's not a great deal of French spoken in Australia.'

'Then it's time we diversified, got away from sewing machines and sheepskins out there. I think we should be considering openings in Europe.'

Hector, sitting beside me, choked back a derisive noise. Gregory opened his round eyes wide, apparently astounded at any business initiative from his son.

'I'm glad to hear you taking an interest, Ben, but this sort of thing needs a great deal of discussion.'

'Oh, I'm not suggesting anything too ambitious to start with. Something like this for instance.'

He flipped the paper across the table to his father. Gregory stared at it and passed it to me. For the second time in an hour I found myself translating the property advertisement. The rest of the family listened with furrowed brows. At the end of it Hector said: 'I don't quite see what it has to do with us.'

'Madame Martin's idea. Bon-bons and buttonholes for the boulevardiers of Geneva. With the right management it could hardly fail.'

Gregory's lips were twitching and you could see that another bout of nervous indigestion wasn't far away.

'You'll find it's not easy to get the right management, especially in a foreign country.'

'Oh, Sylvie Martin would run it. I'm sure she'd be first-rate.'

Until then, Beatrice had taken no part in the conversation, apart from glancing from one to the other of

51

them, trying to keep up. But it seemed a characteristic of hers that her remarks, when they did come, were placed for maximum impact. Into the brief silence that followed Ben's words she dropped another of her conversational silver spoons.

'I should think Mademoiselle Martin would be better at running quite a different sort of establishment.'

As it tinkled delicately on the floor we all gaped at her, not sure that we'd heard aright. Then Ben broke the silence with a great rip of laughter.

'Oh, my dear sister, I didn't think you knew about these things.'

Whether Beatrice had meant her remark in the sense that he'd taken it, I don't know. She sat there, red flooding into her cheeks and tears gathering in her eyes. Hector rounded on Ben.

'You're a complete barbarian. You shouldn't be allowed—'

'Well, if Bea's going to pass judgement on a woman she hardly knows and imply—'

Gregory glared at both of them.

'If you think this is a suitable subject—'

'Oh, be quiet all of you. Be quiet. Be quiet. Be quiet.'

Beatrice jumped up, hands on her ears and tears streaming down her face, and ran out of the room.

'Now look what you've done,' said Hector to Ben.

Gregory gave one of his delicate little burps and put a hand hastily to his mouth, his round eyes staring out miserably over it. Feet pounded upstairs and a door slammed.

'I'd better go to her,' Hector said.

If Gregory objected to this assumption of a fiancé's duties, he was in no position to do anything about it. Hector went upstairs and we heard him knocking gently on the door and calling to her. He was back a few minutes later.

'She says she's lying down and doesn't want to talk to anyone.'

All in all, it was a relief to get back to an afternoon of

undertakers and funeral arrangements. Gregory's presence wasn't essential so we persuaded him to go to his room and rest. Hector was subdued as we walked to the mayor's office together.

'I suppose he'll spend the afternoon reading that journal. I don't suppose it will help matters, do you?'

'No.'

'But it's Ben causing the real problems. Can you understand the man, going to such trouble to annoy his father? How on earth did he get hold of that advertisement for a shop of all things?'

'I don't think there's any great mystery about that. He got it from Sylvie Martin.'

He looked even more worried.

'I've been thinking about what you were saying, about Arthur causing the accident.'

'I only said he might have. It was no more than a guess.'

'All too accurate, I'd say, in view of what's happened.'

'But what exactly has happened, apart from . . . ?'

'Apart from another Mordiford mealtime, you mean? No wonder poor Gregory gets indigestion. Well, let's assume that Uncle Arthur was in some way responsible for making Madame a widow. If so, she presumably thinks the family owes her something.'

'After thirty years?'

'She hasn't had a chance before, has she? Gregory wouldn't have come near the place if it hadn't been for the reappearance of Uncle Arthur.'

'Even if she suspects something about the accident she couldn't prove it.'

'No. It would simply be a matter of applying pressure on poor Gregory. It looks to me as if they're rather good at it. They've found one weak point already, namely Ben. I don't think he really wants to do his father any harm, but he never considers.'

By this time I was feeling subdued as well. If there were some kind of Martin family plot, that would explain why Pierre had been so anxious to have my opinion about the journal. I didn't like the thought of that, or the feeling that

I was being trapped between Martins and Mordifords. We were almost at the mayor's office before Hector sighed and answered the question I'd put some time ago.

'So I'm afraid what's happened is that the Martin family have just presented their bill.'

SEVEN

DINNER THAT EVENING, WITH BOTH families present, was calm though on the gloomy side. Gregory looked no worse than at lunchtime, so at least reading the journal didn't seem to have increased his misery. Beatrice was moist-eyed and suffering from a headache and I could see that Hector was concerned about her. Everything went formally to the very end of the meal. The maids began to clear away dessert plates and coffee-cups. Madame Martin got up to leave and Hector rose politely to open the door for her. When he sat down again he must have left it ajar because, as I watched, a black twitching nose appeared round it, then a paw hooked it open and a medium-sized dog, more like a collie than anything, came trotting into the room and made for Pierre at the far end of the table. It had the half-triumphant, half-apprehensive air of an animal that's managed to get where it shouldn't be. Pierre made reproachful noises but fondled its head.

'Ah, the guide's sagacious dog.'

The comment came from Hector. I turned to look at him, trying to remember why the words were familiar, and found his eyes on me. Then it struck me that I'd read them the night before in the journal and I couldn't keep the surprise from my face. 'The guide's sagacious dog' had gone with the party on the first day of their holiday. The chances of Hector's choosing that particular adjective were so slender that I knew he'd set a trap for me and by showing my surprise I'd fallen into it. He'd somehow suspected that I'd seen his uncle's journal and wanted to confirm it. The question was how he'd managed to see it

55

himself. To the best of my knowledge it had gone straight from me to Gregory, via Madame Martin. The only explanation seemed to be that Gregory had shown him the journal, then I glanced across at Gregory and saw an expression of surprise on his face even greater than mine. More than surprise – an embarrassment amounting to horror.

It felt as if we were all frozen there for minutes on end, but I don't suppose it lasted for more than a second or two. When I recovered Pierre was still petting the dog, gently pulling its ears. Beatrice, sitting next to her father, asked him if he felt ill. He smiled weakly and put a hand to his chest.

'Just my old trouble I'm afraid, my dear. Please don't worry, I'll take myself upstairs. If somebody would kindly send me up a glass of hot water . . .'

'I'll boil up some in your room, or a cup of weak china tea. I'm glad we brought the spirit stove.'

He went across the room in small steps, hand on Beatrice's arm as if afraid of falling. Hector offered to go up with them, but he insisted he could manage. When he'd gone Hector caught my eye and glanced towards the door. I followed him downstairs to the bench beside the geraniums.

'Well, Miss Bray, did you find my uncle's journal interesting?'

'As interesting as you did, apparently. I thought it odd at the time that a man as efficient as you seem to be should forget something so obvious as his employer's passport.'

He wasn't in the least put out. I sensed a new relationship between us, a kind of conspiracy.

'It was the only chance I had to read it before Uncle did. After all, I didn't have your advantage of being there when they picked it out of the glacier.'

He was assuming, naturally enough, that I'd read the whole thing then. I didn't correct him.

'Why did you want to read it first?'

'For the same reason that I came to you for some idea of what his body looked like. It's a bad time for poor

Gregory. I see it as my business to protect him as much as I can.'

'Was that why you chose that very public way of letting him know you'd read it?'

'Yes. If I'd told him in private he'd have had to discuss it there and then. This way he has a night to sleep on it before deciding on his line. He is the boss, you know. That might not be the impression you've had of him, but Gregory's the man who decides.'

'Decides what, exactly?'

'How much he rattles the family skeleton. Better unrattled, wouldn't you think?'

'Since it isn't my family's skeleton, it's hardly my business.'

He smiled, a nice open smile.

'You don't really expect to keep to that, do you? Not with your particular talents.'

I wasn't flattered and I let him see it. It was fair enough that he'd made inquiries about me on the English gossip circuit before employing my services. A couple of prison terms and a record of political agitation were not things I tried to hide. But it sounded as if he'd been hearing about other things that were really none of my fault.

'What particular talents of mine had you in mind, Mr Tenby?'

'Brrr.'

'What?'

'I feel as if I'd just run full tilt into a snowdrift. I wasn't trying to offend you. I should have thought you'd be proud of your detective talents.'

'I lay no claim to detective talents. It's just a matter of trying to keep reasonably clear-minded.'

'And you're applying clear-mindedness to this business of Uncle Arthur. Is that why you decided to take a moonlight walk with Monsieur Martin?'

'Oh, it was you at the window, was it?'

'No, Ben, as a matter of fact. But he made sure I knew about it as soon as I got up this morning. He seemed to think it was very amusing. Naturally I told him gentlemen

57

didn't bandy ladies' names over the shaving soap and threw him out.'

'Very chivalrous.'

'It did cross my mind to defend you by saying you were only doing it to ask him about our unfortunate occurrence. That was the reason, wasn't it?'

I didn't answer.

'As a matter of interest, did Monsieur Mordiford throw any light on the question?'

'Not much. There was an avalanche. It happened in the early morning, as they should have been getting ready to leave the Grands Mulets hut.'

'Did he know what caused it? I want to know if there are any more unpleasant surprises in line for Uncle Gregory.'

'Not for certain, but I'm afraid what he told me makes it more likely that Arthur was doing something stupid.'

I gave him Pierre's account of the night and early morning at the hut.

'There was no good reason for your uncle to be down there on the snow on his own. It sounds as if he went wandering off for some reason and the avalanche happened when Pierre's father was trying to get him back.'

He looked down at the cobbles and sighed.

'I was afraid of something like that.'

'Of course, we know now that he was probably in a confused state of mind at the time.'

'That quotation in the journal, you mean? At least I assume it's a quotation, Marlowe or Webster or somebody vengeful like that.'

'Dr Johnson.'

'Who do you think put it there?'

'There must be four possibilities, including Arthur himself.'

'Why would he do it?'

'He might have found out something about a woman he thought he could trust.'

'Or one of the other three might have found out something.'

His voice, usually cheerful, was flat and depressed.

'If it was one of the others, wouldn't you say the most likely one would be . . . well, his brother?'

'I don't know your Uncle Gregory well, but he strikes me as quite a worldly character. Whoever wrote that in the journal must have been a narrow-minded and censorious man.'

'But young men are censorious, aren't they, and it's a long time ago. If Gregory did it, that would explain one thing that's been puzzling me.'

'What?'

'Why he's so determined to bring Arthur home to bury him. A kind of atonement, perhaps.'

We sat in silence for a while, with the light fading.

'Miss Bray, I'd take it as a kindness if you wouldn't say anything to the others about this. The way Ben's behaving to his father at present, there's no telling what he might say to him. As for Beatrice, the poor girl's developing a morbid interest in Arthur's fiancée in any case. This would make matters worse.'

I said I wouldn't. As he held the door for me to go in he said: 'By the bye, did anything odd strike you about the first day of the journal?'

'The Day of the Sagacious Dog. No. Why?'

'Just a thought.'

I said good-night to Hector in the hall and went straight upstairs. I slept well and only woke as the first light was coming through my attic window. It was early but I could hear noises coming from downstairs, probably the maids at work already. The bathroom was on the landing below mine so I gathered up towel and sponge bag and tiptoed down to it. Not a sound was coming from behind the closed doors of the Mordifords. As I was going back up to my room I paused by the landing window, watching the sun hit the sides of the Aiguilles Rouges. Then a movement directly below caught my eye, down in the little courtyard. Two people were standing there. I could only see the tops of their heads but one of them was immediately recognisable from her white hair and round lace cap as Madame Martin. The other was a man in a

59

panama. Until he moved away from the house a little I couldn't be sure who he was. Once he moved, there was no doubt of it. Gregory Mordiford. No reason, of course, why he shouldn't be chatting with his hostess in the garden, except that six o'clock in the morning seemed an odd time to do it.

Gregory came down to breakfast two hours later with a determined air about him. This was appropriate because today, if we were lucky, would see the end of the form-filling and he'd receive formal permission to take his brother's body home. I was nearly at the end of my work and within the next twenty-four hours, or forty-eight at most, could expect to collect my fee and wave the Mordifords on their way. If they took some unanswered questions with them as well as a body, that should be no concern of mine. Beatrice must have been thinking along the same lines. As she crumbled her croissant she said something about needing to start packing. Quietly, Gregory delivered his bombshell.

'I think we may not travel until Friday after all. There are some things I want to discuss with Madame Martin.'

His children and nephew stared at him, amazed. Ben was the first to speak.

'Business discussions, Father?'

'Yes. I've decided that on reflection there may be a lot to be said for her idea of opening a shop in Geneva. She's a surprisingly sensible and businesslike woman.'

Hector's eyes met mine. The expression in them said, 'He's accepted her bill.'

Ben drawled: 'I do hope it won't upset you too much to hear me say it, Father, but I think that's a very good idea.'

If not upset, Gregory certainly didn't seem too pleased at praise from this quarter.

'There will be conditions, Ben, and you and I will have to discuss them, but not over the breakfast table.'

Beatrice had dropped her croissant and was nibbling at a fingernail instead. She looked at her father as if she couldn't believe what she was hearing.

'Are you sure it's the right time to make the decision,

Father? Perhaps if you were to wait until we get home . . .'

Her voice trailed away as she saw the expression on his face. He was kindly enough, but it was clear he was taking no notice of her.

'With Miss Bray's help we shall finish what has to be done at the mayor's office today. Then on Thursday we shall go to see the place where poor Arthur's body was found.'

The expression on Ben's face showed what he thought of that, but he said nothing. After all, he'd got his way about the shop. It was Hector who protested, though gently.

'Are you sure that's a good idea? Don't you think you've done enough in that line?'

I agreed with him. These pieties were having a bad effect on Gregory's health and the more I knew about Arthur's death the more convinced I became that he shouldn't rake the bones more than the ice had raked them already.

'It was Madame Martin's suggestion and she is very kindly making the arrangements. It would be discourteous to her to refuse.'

Nothing more was said about it as Gregory, Hector and I took our familiar route through the town. Gregory walked faster than usual and said little, eager to get things finished. By mid-afternoon we had collected our last set of stamps and signatures and received permission to take Arthur Mordiford's mortal remains back to the soil of his ancestors. All we had to do now was to take the forms to the undertaker and he would do the rest. I began to hurry our party, as gently as I could, towards the *pompes funèbres* workshop in a back street but Gregory insisted on going back to the Maison Martin first. He said it wouldn't be long so we waited for him outside in the sun. When he came out there was a bulge in his jacket pocket and he was carrying a familiar brown paper parcel.

'I've decided that Arthur's things should go into the coffin with him. If you could explain that to the undertaker, Miss Bray, I'd be very grateful.'

The undertaker, a small brown man with a drooping

61

moustache, was impressed by the story of the long-dead Englishman and professionally proud of his involvement. Thanks to the mayor's office the body was already on its way from the mortuary and the cart drew up outside while we were in the workshop. We drank coffee in a dark little office, with muffled sounds from next door, as the undertaker and his assistants settled it into the substantial coffin that Gregory had chosen. At last we were called into the workshop to see their handiwork. A linen shroud covered the body, nestled into a surround of black crêpe. The undertaker had drawn the material low over the forehead, hiding the gash. Gregory produced the watch and the broken ice-axe from their parcel and they were carefully tucked alongside. We stood for a minute in silence. The undertaker and his assistants waited respectfully, the coffin lid propped against the wall.

'And this.'

Gregory produced from his pocket a rectangular object wrapped in waterproof cloth. The journal. Hector made a sound that might have been the beginning of a protest, soon checked. The undertaker took it and we watched as it was tucked beside the body and the lid lowered. It was almost unbearably hot and heavy in the workshop, the smell of wood shavings mingling with mortuary chemicals, and I expected us to go once the lid was down. But Gregory waited until the last brass screw was fastened and the last seal pressed into thick black wax, as the regulations demanded. Then he thanked the undertaker, shook hands with him and led the way out into the sunshine with the air of duty thoroughly done.

EIGHT

OUTSIDE THE MAISON MARTIN AT ten o'clock on Thursday morning I felt a tap on my shoulder and turned to find myself looking at a grey whiskery face with teeth bared and ears back.

'Your mule, mademoiselle.'

'I'm walking, thank you.'

I'd been standing back watching the final preparations for the memorial pilgrimage to the Glacier des Bossons. Gregory Mordiford and Marie Martin were already mounted on their mules. She was dressed in her usual black silk with the addition of a primrose-coloured sunshade and seemed to be in her element, overseeing everything like a general at the start of a campaign. Sylvie and the maids were sent flying in and out of the house for last minute essentials – a tin of wafer biscuits, fruit knives, oil of citronella for keeping off the insects. The baggage mules were already so loaded with food, drink and wooden picnic chairs that they looked like market stalls on spindly legs.

Beatrice came out, neat in blue hat and dress but looking anxious. She was carrying kettle, spirit stove and teapot and stared unhappily at the loaded mules.

'Is there space for these?'

With nobody else taking any notice she repeated the question to her brother who was lounging beside the door pretending not to notice the circus going on round him.

'What in the world do you want those for? There's plenty of wine and lemonade.'

'Tea's better For father's digestion.'

63

Hector saw her predicament, took the things and managed to strap them precariously on to one of the mule-saddles. Pierre was giving the mule-boys their orders. Beyond a polite but distant good morning he'd had little to say to any of us. I guessed that this expedition was beneath his dignity as a mountain guide, as well as against his better judgement.

Sylvie said something to her mother then took her place lightly on the smallest and palest of the mules. She was looking particularly attractive in a white dress with a pleated bodice and straw hat trailing long blue ribbons. Ben detached himself from the door post and obviously intended to help her settle herself in the saddle but she glanced at him, bit her lip and shook her head. He turned away, looking furious, and when we set out at last up the street he was trailing a long way behind.

'I do hope Ben's not going to make trouble.'

Hector, like me, had chosen to walk. We were near the head of our long procession as it wound through the town, just behind Pierre and his dog.

'Have he and Mademoiselle Martin quarrelled?'

'You noticed? No, I don't think they've quarrelled, it's just that she's got more business sense than he has. You see, Uncle's decision to finance their confectionery shop wasn't entirely without conditions.'

'Conditions affecting Ben?'

'Indirectly. I gather he let Madame Martin know that he'd reconsider the whole thing if there were to be any cause for anxiety between those two. Naturally Madame won't run the risk of everything falling through because of that and nor will her daughter.'

'Does Ben know?'

'I'm not sure of that.'

'Your uncle must have been very worried.'

'Yes. It might even have been in his mind that Ben would up and marry her.'

Our progress was stately, first along the main valley road, then up a path that climbed between scrubby little willow trees, the warm air full of bees and butterflies.

Then it rose more steeply into pinewoods and the mules padded softly over a carpet of dead brown needles, the warm smell of sap rising round us. As we rounded hairpin bends we could see the riders and the baggage mules curling in a long line below us. At about midday we stopped for a coffee at a little chalet in the woods beside the Cascade du Dard. There were chairs and tables on the terrace overlooking the pinewoods and you had to raise your voice to be heard over the thunder of the waterfall. The boys stayed outside with their mules while we arranged ourselves round two tables. Madame Martin and Gregory kept themselves a little apart from the rest and talked in low voices. Beatrice watched them, fiddling nervously with her white gloves and the clip of her parasol. Her nails were so badly bitten that the flesh beside them was red and raw.

'Where's Ben?'

The question came suddenly from Gregory. Beatrice jumped as if somebody had threatened to hit her. Since he wasn't out on the path with the mules there was only one place he could be. There was a viewing platform round the corner of the chalet, for people who wanted a closer view of the waterfall, and Gregory made for it at a fast walk, Beatrice trailing after him. Hector caught my eye and we followed.

The viewing platform stands above a blue-green pool, with the stream pouring itself into it, straight as milk from a jug. Steps lead from the platform down to a little bridge across the stream below the pool. When we got to the platform there were two people on the bridge, staring at the fall of water. Sylvie and Ben. There was a little distance between them but as we watched Ben made a sudden move towards her that was clearly an attempt to grab her hand. It looked to me as if he were trying to ask her some urgent question. She pulled away so abruptly that she dropped her parasol into the stream. It stuck under the bridge for a moment then went sailing away. As she turned she saw us, gave a gasp and came running past us, up the steps and across the platform with a set and angry expression on her face.

'Benedict, come here. Come at once.'

Gregory's shout must have been audible on the bridge, even over the noise of the waterfall, but Ben took his time.

'Benedict, I've warned you. I will not have you behaving like this.'

'Like what, Governor?'

His father took him by the arm and practically frog-marched him back to the café tables.

Hector and I brought Beatrice back at a slower pace. She was more upset by the incident than seemed reasonable and shaking with anger against Sylvie.

'Oh, that awful woman. That awful woman.'

Hector tried to point out tactfully that Ben had made the first move.

'Only because she's been leading him on. They're witches, awful French witches, both of them. Look how they're making poor Father give money to them for this shop. Oh, I wish we were back at home.'

Her voice rose in a wail. We sat her down, as far from Marie and Sylvie as we could. Hector patted her hands while I went to fetch lemonade for her.

When I came out Ben was sitting on his own, managing to get great clouds of defiant smoke out of a small cheroot, and Gregory had joined Beatrice and Hector. His anger with Ben seemed to have left a residue of depression and he didn't say much as we walked back to the line of mules. Pierre was waiting beside them, looking impatient. If he knew what had been happening at the café he gave no sign of it. I'd had enough of Mordiford emotional storms so when the procession started again I walked with him at the front. As I walked, I revised my ideas. The censorious Gregory I'd just seen, reacting out of all proportion to the sight of his grown-up son responding to an attractive woman, seemed very close to the man who might have scored an insulting quote in his brother's journal. The path became steeper and stonier and the first ice-blocks at the edge of the glacier were in sight. Even the sure-footed mules stumbled on loose stones and were cursed or encouraged upwards by the boys. We went on until we came to a wide patch of grass merging into grey rocks with the glacier on the far side.

'We stop here.'

It was as far as the mules would go and as good a site for the picnic as any. The idea seemed to be that the women should organise the picnic while the men completed their pilgrimage on foot to the place where Arthur's body had been found. I was annoyed by this and had intended to add myself to the men's party until Hector came over to me.

'Would you keep an eye on Beatrice for me please, Nell? I don't like leaving her on her own with Madame and Sylvie.'

I agreed. I stood beside her and waved them off as they went up the path on foot, first Pierre, then Gregory, then Hector. Ben, as usual, trailed a long way behind. I don't think he'd have joined them at all except that his father said a few sharp words to him as they set off. He had the air of a rebuked schoolboy, pretending not to care.

Madame was arranging the picnic. A line of mule-boys scurried with chairs, bottles and baskets. Sylvie spread a shining white linen cloth on the grass and began to arrange a pyramid of fruit in the middle of it. Since Beatrice couldn't stand the sight of either of them without looking as if she wanted to be sick I tried to distract her by taking her for a closer look at the ice. She shuddered.

'Do you think she came up here?'

'Who?'

'That poor woman who was engaged to Uncle Arthur.'

Daisy Whatwashername seemed to have sunk deeply into her imagination.

'I wrote a poem about her last night, wandering through the snow, looking for him.'

Given the slightest encouragement, she'd probably start reciting it.

'I shouldn't have thought she'd get above the snowline in summer, unless she was a particularly strong walker.'

She gave me a look that condemned me as a

67

literal-minded philistine, but at least the danger of recitation receded. She stood for a long time looking out at the ice-blocks, probably turning another poem over in her head, until I suggested that we should walk up the path a little way to meet Hector and the others coming down. As we went she said:

'Father won't let me marry Hector, you know, because Ben has made him so angry with that awful woman.'

I said he surely wouldn't be so unreasonable, but she seemed set on a career as a tragic fiancée.

'It's made him seem so cold, having to come out here and think about Uncle Arthur. I wish he'd stayed frozen in the ice, never come down.'

About half a mile on we heard stones rattling and men's voices above us, hushed and anxious. When the party came in sight round a bend Beatrice cried out and I was shocked too at the sight of Gregory. The inspection of a dip in the ice where his brother had been seemed to have had a worse effect on him than the corpse itself. He moved like a man in a daze and seemed to have aged ten years in an hour. His eyes were flooded with tears and when he looked down and saw Beatrice he screwed his head aside as if he didn't want his daughter to see his misery. Pierre walked a step in front of him, turned sideways on and ready to catch him if he stumbled. Hector came close behind with Ben following, sulky but more subdued.

Between us we got him to the picnic place where Madame Martin and Sylvie were waiting and sat him down on one of the folding chairs. He insisted he was all right, although he obviously wasn't, accepted a glass of claret and sipped. Beatrice decided that what he needed was tea and made a great business of finding and setting up the kettle and spirit stove. This involved several trips to and from the mules for pieces of gear, then she found she'd forgotten matches.

'Oh dear. Could you . . .'

Kneeling in the grass she glanced from me to the drooping figure of her father. A bitten fingernail went to her mouth and she seemed near to tears. Hastily I said I'd

68

see to it and got a box from Hector. He had a hand on his uncle's shoulder but his eyes were on Beatrice, drooped over her kettle like a mourning nymph over an urn.

'Look after her. Tell her I'll be with her in a minute.'

Gregory didn't even look up. Ben was standing on the other side of his father, looking quite concerned about him for once. I took the matches back to Beatrice and stayed with her until the kettle had boiled and the tea was brewing. Hector strolled across to us.

'He says he thinks he could drink a cup of tea, with a slice of lemon.'

'Lemon.'

Her fingernail went to her mouth again. She stared round distractedly. I remembered seeing a net of oranges and lemons loaded on the mules and suggested we should go over and look for them. Hector gave me a grateful glance. I guessed he was torn between the need to look after Beatrice and keep Gregory from fretting at the same time. When we came back with lemons and a knife he had a cup of tea already poured.

'Is it too strong, do you think?'

He handed me the cup and I took a gulp, burning my mouth.

'Yes, a bit strong for a delicate digestion.'

Beatrice poured another half cup and looked round for the kettle of hot water to dilute it. There were only a few drops left in the kettle but Hector, a little impatient by now, said it would have to do. I hacked a slice off a lemon and Beatrice carried the cup carefully across to her father, sitting beside him on the grass while he drank. I finished off the other cup, Hector standing beside me.

'What happened up there?'

'I'll tell you later. It turned out to be worse than he expected.'

'He looks shaken.' A thought struck me. 'You didn't find the other foot, did you?'

'No, nothing like that.'

He was trying to be calm but there was a nerviness about him. Something had happened up there that had affected

69

all four of them. Pierre was sitting at some distance away from the rest of the party, his back against a rock and his face towards the ice. His air warned off interruptions.

'We'll let Uncle have a rest here, then I want to get him down as soon as possible. I never thought this was a good idea.'

We went over to join the picnic and I ate and drank hurriedly, a chunk of bread and pâté, washed down with some gulps of red wine. Gregory ate nothing, in spite of Beatrice's urgings, and said little. From time to time he glanced at his watch and then down to the valley, as if late for an appointment. But when Pierre got up and came towards him he seemed almost scared. His hand went to his mouth to hide a burp and his round miserable eyes stared at Pierre over his fingers.

'If you feel well enough, we should start our journey down.'

There was something odd about Pierre's manner, though I couldn't quite place it. It was as if he had an authority over Gregory that hadn't been there before. Gregory nodded, stood up and winced, hand on his ribs.

'Poor Father, your indigestion again?'

He nodded and sat back on the chair. Madame Martin was decisive.

'A glass of Gentian will help.'

She took a full bottle from a basket and broke the wax seal on it with the gesture of a farmer's wife wringing a chicken's neck. Sylvie brought a small glass, held it for her mother to fill and gave it to Gregory. He sipped weakly at first then seemed to gather strength and finished off the glass.

While this was going on the rest of us were packing up for the downward trek, hastily and without much care. The urge to get down the mountain as soon as possible had become a passion. Hector collected cups and plates into a basket, Beatrice emptied her teapot into the grass and even Ben tried to make himself useful, taking the basket containing glasses and Gentian bottle from one of the overburdened mule-boys. Ben, Beatrice and Hector

70

converged on one pack mule at the same time. Sylvie arrived, bearing fruit and tried to explain to them in French that they weren't loading it properly. Beatrice, catching the drift if not the words, told Sylvie to be quiet and go away. Among the four of them they managed to drop the basket. It fell to the stony path with a smashing of glass and the smell of alcohol hit the air as the Gentian began sinking back into the soil from which long roots had sucked it.

'Now look what you've done,' said Beatrice to Sylvie.

By the time they'd all calmed down the boys had finished the packing and Gregory seemed well enough to be helped on to his mule. He walked steadily enough, although there was still a dazed look about him. Pierre walked in front of the mule, Hector beside it and I followed. For the first ten minutes or so it looked as if we might be past the worst, but suddenly Gregory slumped in his saddle, made an incoherent sound and put a hand to his throat. Alarmed, we got him off the mule as quickly as we could. He almost fell into Pierre's arms and we propped him up beside the path with his back against a rock. The rest of the party came to a halt behind us. Beatrice came scrambling down the path on foot, face white.

'What's happening now?'

Hector put an arm round her and gently steered her to one side. Pierre bounded towards a stream for water while I commandeered Madame's primrose parasol to make a shade for Gregory.

When Pierre came with the water Gregory sipped some of it, but his face contorted and he fell back against the rock.

'Burning. It feels as if it's burning.'

His hand went to his throat again. Pierre offered more water, holding the cup to his mouth. He gulped it greedily, slopped it and seemed to be trying to apologise, but his speech was becoming slurred and his eyes weren't focusing. Pierre stood up, his face serious, and sent one of the mule-boys running back down the path to the chalet.

'Ask them to send somebody down to the town for a doctor, or signal if they can. Tell them it's urgent.'

The boy ran. Gregory's breathing became laboured. He was trying hard to say something but his voice broke down into painful gulpings. I knelt down to try to understand what he meant.

'Ben. Get Ben.'

That was what it sounded like. I called for Ben and he was there almost at once. He looked down at his father, face both scared and disgusted, and it seemed to take an effort of will for him to kneel beside Gregory. When his father's hand shot out and grabbed the lapel of his white linen jacket he looked as if he wanted to pull away.

'Ben . . .'

His eyes rolled. He twisted sideways, still gripping Ben's lapel and was violently sick into the grass. Then his fingers relaxed and he fell unconscious. Without a word Pierre scooped him into his arms and set off at a run down the path. I followed, with Hector close behind and the rest goodness knows where. Just above the chalet we met a party coming up with a stretcher, but by then Gregory Mordiford was dead.

NINE

'DID THEY SAY IT WAS POISON?'

Ben repeated the question, leaning forward in his chair. 'Did they definitely say it was poison?'

It was late at night in the upstairs dining-room, with only Ben, Hector and myself there. None of us could even summon up the energy to switch on the lights so we sat in near darkness, apart from a small lamp on the sideboard. We were all three of us tired to the point of unconsciousness, Ben and Hector from their sessions with the authorities, I from trying to calm Beatrice. She was asleep at last upstairs from the effects of a sleeping draught the doctor had prescribed. While I sat beside her bed waiting for it to work she kept coming back to the belief that the family's return to Chamonix had some kind of curse attached to it. Then there was her hatred of the two Martin women. From the time Hector broke it to her that her father was dead, she hadn't wavered in her belief that they'd poisoned him. She'd tried to fly at Sylvie Martin up at the chalet in the woods and the two parties had to come down the mountain separately, the Martins first, then the Mordifords. Now Hector and Ben were comparing notes about what they'd learned from the police.

'No, they didn't say in so many words that it was poison, or if they did the interpreter didn't pass it on. But it was obvious from the questions – what he ate, what he drank.'

'What did you tell them?'

'That as far as I knew he hadn't eaten anything since breakfast. There was a coffee at the place by the waterfall,

73

then various things to drink at lunch . . .'

'The gentian stuff.'

'. . . A cup of tea, some wine and, yes, the Gentian.'

'Nobody else drank that.'

'Nobody else drank the tea either,' Ben said.

I'd have liked to let it all drift over me, but I had to come in there.

'I drank a whole cup of it.'

'And you're still here.'

Ben didn't sound particularly pleased about that. Hector said wearily: 'That's it then, the Gentian.'

Without asking us if we minded Ben lit one of his cigarillos and took a long draw on it.

'Aren't we ruling out something?'

We both stared at him.

'What?'

'The possibility that my father killed himself.'

Hector made a disbelieving noise. I said I'd only known Gregory for a few days but he hadn't struck me as a man contemplating suicide.

'That is, not until . . .'

I didn't finish the sentence. Ever since we came down from the glacier I'd tried to tell myself that it was no business of mine.

'Except what, Miss Bray?'

'Well, you couldn't help seeing that there was a change in him after the four of you had been up to see the place where the body was. Did something happen up there?'

It was too dark to see if they were looking at each other, but I could feel some kind of signal pass between these two men who weren't usually in sympathy.

'Yes, something happened,' Hector said at last.

'What?'

'We got up to the place without any trouble. Ben decided that he didn't want to come any further and said he'd have a smoke and wait for us on the path. Gregory, Pierre and I went on.'

'There wasn't much to see, was there?'

'No. You could see where he'd been chipped out, but nothing there to upset Gregory so badly. I went back and sat on the grass, but Gregory and Pierre were standing by the ice for quite a while. I think Pierre was pointing out the route the body might have come down. When they came back to us, Grégory was nearly crying, wasn't he, Ben?'

'I didn't see.'

'So it was after his conversation with Pierre that he seemed so shocked?'

'Yes. Perhaps Pierre said something tactless without meaning to. His English isn't perfect and Gregory must have been in a worse state by then than any of us realised. I always thought the trip was a bad idea, but then he wouldn't offend Madame Martin.'

Silence. The Martins must be somewhere in the tall house but we'd seen nothing of them since we came down separately from the mountain. The maids had served a kind of dinner that nobody wanted. Hector got up to open a window, letting out some of the cigarillo smoke.

'You know the procedure better than we do, Miss Bray. What happens next?'

'I suppose the examining magistrate will be called in tomorrow. He'll want to speak to all of us.'

More silence. Ben said slowly: 'That would mean they think it was deliberate.'

'That they think there was a possibility of it, yes.'

'That's hardly a surprise, is it, Ben?'

All the brash confidence seemed to have gone out of Ben, as if only his father's life had fuelled it. He mumbled something inaudible and had to repeat it.

'Will they want to talk to Beatrice?'

'They can't. Beatrice isn't well enough to speak to anybody, is she, Miss Bray?'

'She's certainly hardly coherent. If she goes in front of an examining magistrate or anybody else in authority she's almost certain to blurt out that Marie or Sylvie Martin poisoned her father.'

Plus, quite probably, mad fiancées and family curses, though I didn't say that.

Hector, deliberate as ever, was following up his chain of thought.

'The examining magistrate will want a lot of background to things, what we were doing here and so on.'

'He probably knows already if he lives in the town, but he'd need to confirm it for the record.'

'The question is, how much we tell him.'

He was talking to me, not to Ben.

'About what?'

'The journal and so on. Family skeletons.'

Ben didn't react at all.

'Is it relevant to how your uncle died?'

'I don't see how it can be. And it would upset Beatrice even more if it got out about that quotation. If there's even any possibility that Gregory wrote it . . .'

Would it add to her worries so greatly that her father might have been guilty of a piece of meanness years before she was born? Difficult to say with Beatrice, and Hector should know her better than anybody.

'I'll only mention it if it's obviously relevant.'

No more than a half-promise, but he'd have to be content with that.

Soon afterwards Ben yawned loudly and said he was going up to bed. Hector said good-night too, but lingered at the door.

'I'm sorry we seem to have dragged you into this, Miss Bray.'

I was sorry too.

'No help for it. I'll look in on Beatrice on the way upstairs.'

I'd hoped to find her asleep but when I opened the door quietly I heard a scrabbling sound and there she was on her knees in her night-dress, hair loose, bending over something. Her eyes were hazy from the effects of the sleeping draught, but all the tension in her seemed to be fighting against it. I saw that the thing she was bending over was her cardboard box full of flower specimens.

'Somebody's been interfering with them.'

Grief takes odd forms and I thought this was one of

them. I spoke soothingly, suggesting she must be mistaken. She shook her head.

'No. I'd classified them into piles, ready for pressing. They're all mixed up now and some of them have gone.'

'Do you know which ones?'

'Crypripedium calceolus and Aconitum vulparia.'

Venus's sabot and wolf-killer, the two particularly noticed by Sylvie Martin. One way or the other, I thought that was no coincidence.

'When do you think they went?'

'I don't know. They were there yesterday afternoon because that was when I was classifying them. Anybody could have come in since then.'

Which was true enough. There were keys to the rooms, but they usually stayed in the locks or were hung on a board by the bottom of the stairs. I was worried, but still far from convinced. I persuaded her to get back into bed and said I'd go down to the kitchen and bring her up some hot milk.

I was on my way back upstairs with it when I met Sylvie in the passageway, still in her white dress with a blue shawl thrown over it.

'My brother gave me a message for you.'

'What?'

I hadn't seen Pierre since we came down.

'He said you were please not to talk about the book. I don't know what book.'

'Why not? May I speak to him?'

She shook her head.

'He's not here. He's gone back to the mountain.'

'At this time of night? Why?'

She shrugged.

'He does that sometimes, takes his dog and goes. Sometimes my mother and I don't see him for days.'

It was hard to know whether it was tolerance or contempt in the way she said it.

'But now?'

With Gregory dead and a murder investigation almost certain.

'I think Pierre is upset.'

'Of course he is. We're all upset.'

'But it's different for Pierre. He lost a monsieur, just like our father did.'

That aspect of things hadn't struck me till then. Arthur Mordiford had gone up the mountain with Pierre's father and come down dead. Thirty years later, the same thing had happened with brother and son. It was undeniable that Martins were not good for Mordifords.

'He feels he can't face the other guides.'

Or the examining magistrate? And why, in the middle of all this, was he so concerned about the journal? Sylvie said a polite good-night and disappeared into the kitchen. Beatrice drank the milk and slept again, leaving me to go on worrying about it on my own.

TEN

I WAS STILL WORRYING WHEN it came to my turn with the examining magistrate the following afternoon. As the outsider of the party, neither a Martin nor a Mordiford, I was the last to be interviewed, apart from Pierre and Beatrice who was still in a state of nervous prostration. He was a conscientious man, quite young for his post in his early forties, with a pear-shaped head on a slim body and sleek black hair. He spoke with traces of the local accent.

'Monsieur Mordiford appeared to be in good health at the beginning of the day?'

'Reasonably. He was under strain, as you know, because of his brother and he suffered from nervous indigestion, but nothing serious that I know.'

'When did his more serious symptoms develop?'

'None of us realised he was dangerously ill until that last stop on the way down, but he hadn't been well before lunch.'

'Before lunch?'

'Yes. You'll know from the others that he'd gone up to see the place where his brother's body was found on the glacier.'

'Whose suggestion was that?'

'Madame Martin's, I think, but he wanted to do it. But the sight of the place seemed to affect him badly.'

'He was depressed?'

'He looked like a man who'd had a bad shock.'

'What did you do?'

'We all got him to sit down and gave him things to drink.'

'What things?'

'A little tea, a few sips of wine, a glass of Gentian.'

I noticed the gleam in his eye when I said 'Gentian', but he went steadily through the list.

'Did anybody else drink tea?'

'I did, with no ill effects.'

'The wine?'

'Quite a few of us drank from the same bottle, also without ill effects.'

'Gentian?'

'As far as I know, he was the only one who drank that. The seal of the bottle was broken just before his glass was poured.'

He made a note of that, although he must have known it already.

'Who broke the seal?'

'Madame Martin.'

'Did she give the drink to him?'

'I think her daughter Sylvie actually did that.'

'Did you see either of them or anybody else put anything but the drink into the glass?'

'I watched while they were doing it. I'm quite certain that nothing else went in.'

Another note.

'What was the effect when he drank?'

'No immediate effect, except that he seemed a little better if anything.'

The afternoon sun was getting into his eyes. He signed to his clerk to draw down a blind.

'I gather the bottle of Gentian was broken soon after Monsieur Mordiford drank from it.'

'Yes. We were all packing up the picnic in a hurry and everybody was trying to load things on the mules at once.'

'Who was near it when it fell?'

I had to think hard to remember.

'Nearly all the Mordiford family, I think.'

'Not Madame Martin?'

'No. I'm sure of that.'

'And Mr Mordiford's condition became worse on the way down?'

'Much worse, in fact altogether different. At lunch he'd been very shaken, but this time it was obvious that something was physically wrong.'

'Did he say anything about what was wrong with him?'

'He said his throat was burning. He had difficulty speaking. He was trying hard to say something to his son Benedict at the end, but couldn't manage it.'

He didn't make a note this time but he was looking at me very intently.

'Had there been anything in the nature of an argument between Mr Mordiford and his son?'

Now who'd put him on to that tack? Since somebody else must have talked about it there was no point in denying it.

'I'm not sure I'd call it an argument. Mr Mordiford had been annoyed about something his son did on the way up.'

He didn't ask what. Perhaps he knew already. Instead he shifted to a new line of questioning.

'What was the relationship between Monsieur Mordiford and Madame Martin?'

'She was very hospitable. He was grateful and polite to her.'

'Did you ever hear them talking about what had happened to his brother?'

'Not about the accident itself, no.'

This was getting dangerously close to the business of the journal which both Hector and Pierre had asked me not to talk about. If there'd been a direct question I should have had to answer it, whether I liked it or not, but the next thing was equally unwelcome.

'Do you happen to have seen Monsieur Pierre Martin today?'

'No.'

'Do you know where he is?'

'Up the mountains somewhere, I suppose. You know he's a guide?'

I was surprised at myself for being so disingenuous and lying by implication. Pierre wasn't doing his normal work. He'd practically gone into hiding and from the way the examining magistrate was looking at me, he

81

probably knew that.

'Yes, I know he's a guide.'

There was an edge of irritation to his voice, but he didn't ask any more about Pierre. After a few more questions, none of which touched on awkward territory, he thanked me and asked where they could contact me if needed. I gave the address of the pension by the station. The Mordifords, I knew, would be moving out of the Maison Martin and I could hardly billet myself on the family without them.

When I got back to the Maison Martin I found the Mordifords in the process of moving out. A horse taxi was waiting in the street outside with a pony cart behind already piled with luggage. As I crossed the courtyard the front door opened and Hector and Ben came out, supporting Beatrice between them. She was wearing a black serge dress that must have been bought hastily off the peg because it was too big for her and too heavy for the weather. A black veil hung over her pale face.

'Miss Bray, are you coming with us?'

Her voice came out from behind the veil like a groan from a cave.

'Where are you going?'

Hector answered for her.

'The Hôtel du Mont Blanc. Beatrice can't stay here.'

'None of us can stay here. They killed my father.'

Hector and her brother tried to quieten her. There was no sign of Madame Martin or Sylvie, only a scared-eyed maid watching from the front door. I helped them get Beatrice settled in the cab and Ben took the seat opposite her. Hector paused, his foot on the step.

'Where will you go?'

I gave him the pension address too. The Hôtel du Mont Blanc was beyond my purse and my inclination.

'You'll come and see Beatrice as soon as you can, won't you? We're sending for her cousin from England, but she needs a woman's company.'

Fretting at the role they'd prepared for me, I watched them drive away and went into the house. I intended to pack my bags and go, but I couldn't do that without seeing Madame Martin. I asked the maid where I'd find her and she pointed down the corridor towards the kitchen, almost speechless with worry. I went and knocked on the door. Madame Martin's voice told me to come in and when I opened the door I was hit by the last thing I expected: a blast of warm, chocolate-scented air. In spite of death, poisoning and police investigations the family business was still going on.

'You won't mind if I go on working?'

Madame Martin's black silk dress was covered by a long apron, starched and gleaming white, her lace cap replaced by a head dress like a nurse's or a nun's. The temperature in the big kitchen was several degrees warmer than outside, from a long black range with copper pans along it. A wooden table ran down the centre of the room, part of it topped by a marble slab. On the marble part of it dozens of the little chocolate models of Mont Blanc were lined up in orderly rows, looking nude without their sugar topping. The plump maid, eyes pink-rimmed, was pounding something in a mortar.

'We don't intend to be disrespectful, you understand, but the shops must have their supplies by the morning.'

I said I quite understood. The maid tipped pulverised sugar from the mortar into a big copper basin and brought it to Madame Martin for inspection. She dipped her little finger into it, nodded and poured on a precise quantity of warm water from one of the pans on the range.

'Thank you, Jeanne. Now would you please go down to the post office for me and see if those moulds we're waiting for have arrived?'

The maid seemed surprised but took off her apron and went. Madame Martin stirred the icing sugar with a wooden spoon.

'The examining magistrate seems quite certain that he was poisoned.'

I hadn't intended it to come out like that. My idea had been that I'd thank her for her hospitality and decide from her manner whether it was worth asking any questions.

But I sensed more than ever a directness in Madame Martin that wouldn't respond to tiptoeing around.

'They were asking me what he drank.'

'Of course. They think it was in my Gentian.'

The slapping of icing sugar against the bowl didn't vary in its steady rhythm.

'Was it?'

'It might have been.'

'Might have been?'

'Who knows what he put in it, poor man. Or he might simply have taken it out of his pocket and swallowed it as it was.'

She held the spoon over the bowl, watching the drips critically, added a dash more water and went on stirring.

'You think he might have killed himself?'

'Of course.'

'With *tue-loup*?'

'Why *tue-loup*? It could have been anything.'

'His daughter had some in her plant collection.'

She shrugged.

'But why would he kill himself?'

'Perhaps he found out something he didn't like.'

'About his brother?'

'Yes, it could be about his brother.'

She seemed perfectly polite, friendly even, but she wasn't letting down her guard for a moment.

'Was that what you told the examining magistrate?'

'The examining magistrate's a fool. I knew his father. He was a fool too and an old goat into the bargain.'

'I shouldn't rely on this one being a fool.'

She gave the icing sugar a last pounding, set down the bowl and began dipping the chocolate mountains into the icing sugar, peaks first. She didn't even look at what she was doing but when she set them back on their bases the icing sugar ran down exactly in the right shape for snow. They went down one after another, tap, tap, tap as we talked.

'He asked me if you and Mr Mordiford had talked about the accident. I told him not as far as I knew.'

Tap, tap, tap.

'He didn't ask me anything about the journal and I didn't tell him. Pierre left a message asking me not to. Do you know why?'

'I don't know what Pierre was thinking.'

'But you were very anxious that I should see the journal before Mr Mordiford read it, anxious enough to lie to him. Why was that?'

'It was necessary that somebody outside the family should read it before he did, to know it existed.'

'Why necessary?'

Tap, tap.

'There was something about that accident, wasn't there? Somebody was careless.'

'Does the book say that?'

'No, but it shows things weren't right. I think there was a quarrel between Arthur and Gregory over a woman.'

'Oh.'

Did I imagine it or was there the very slightest of delays before the next mountain landed? If so the pace picked up again almost at once.

Neither of us spoke for a while until she remarked quite suddenly and in an ordinary conversational tone: 'I hate the mountains.'

'Because of what happened to your husband?'

'Oh, long before that. I wasn't born here, you see. I grew up in Lyons but we moved when I was sixteen because my father was appointed teacher at the school here. I was quite a pretty girl, I suppose and a curiosity to the young guides because I came from the city. They're attractive to silly girls, those handsome young guides. Within two years of coming here I was married to one of them.' She shrugged. 'And so it went. I'd dream, literally dream, of waking up one morning and finding myself somewhere where there weren't the same mountains closing you in all the time, somewhere with a lake and flat, wide paths where you could walk without stumbling and spoiling your dress.'

'Somewhere like Geneva?'

'Yes, somewhere like Geneva.'

'Your son doesn't seem to feel the same way about mountains.'

'Oh, Pierre takes after his father.'

She said it without bitterness, but without much interest either.

'It's all very well for you people who visit, but can you imagine what it's like in winter with the mountains closing in and never seeing the sky from one week to the next? Even in the dark you can still feel them. And they're close, mountain people. All watching their neighbours, all gossiping.' She came to the last of the mountains and thumped it down on the marble harder than the rest so that a crack opened from base to peak. She made an annoyed sound and was about to throw it away when she caught my eye.

'Would you like it? It's very good chocolate.'

She was right, you could tell that even under the coating of warm icing sugar.

'I'm telling you this so that you understand what I'm going to show you. Somebody should see it or his family will try to deny he wrote it, but I can assure you that he did, and before a witness.'

I stopped in mid-bite, trying to adjust to this change of pace. There was a new determination about her, as if she'd just come to a decision. She wiped her fingers on a cloth, went to a tall cupboard in the corner and brought out a box. I found myself looking at a sheet of paper, ordinary business paper with Gregory Mordiford's name and an office address at the head of it. The address had been scored through, replaced by 'Chamonix'.

I, Gregory Mordiford, do hereby certify that Mademoiselle Sylvie Martin, daughter of Madame Marie Martin of Chamonix, is the daughter of my late brother, Arthur Mordiford. In recognition of this, and believing that it would be in accordance with the wishes of my late brother, I undertake to give Miss Martin without conditions the sum of two thousand pounds, this to be binding upon my executors if I die without carrying it out.

86

The date was Wednesday's, the day before he died. It was witnessed by Hector Tenby.

'The stars,' I said.

I was seeing them.

'What stars?'

'In Arthur's journal. I guessed it was when they . . . I mean, I knew it was a love affair, but I thought with his fiancée next door, but all the time it was you and he . . .'

I was staring at her shamelessly, trying to look through thirty years of widowhood to a warm-blooded woman, pining for broad paths and sunshine. Had she hoped that Arthur would take her away to them?

'Yes. He and I.'

Her calm voice was a rebuke to me. I looked again at the paper.

'Why are you showing me?'

'Will it be valid still? For Sylvie's sake.'

'I don't know. I'd normally advise you to ask a lawyer, but as things are . . .'

'Exactly. As things are.'

Gregory poisoned, quite probably in a drink she'd made, the day after writing it.

'But somebody must know, for Sylvie's sake. Nobody respectable would marry her, you see, because of the gossip.'

It was as close as she'd come to pleading with me. I felt angry with Arthur for what he'd done to both of them.

'So you waited thirty years for this?'

'I had no chance before. How could I go to England and ask him? When the body came down, I saw it was the only way to get what was owing to Sylvie.'

This was further proof to me that Gregory had known what was going on thirty years ago. Otherwise he would never have accepted Madame Martin's insistence that Sylvie was his long lost niece.

'No wonder he was so angry about Sylvie and Ben.'

I knew from Hector that he was opposed to the idea of cousins marrying. Seeing his son apparently rushing down that road must have infuriated him, especially if respect for his brother's memory meant he couldn't tell Ben the truth.

There was a commotion in the passage outside. Quick as the beat of a butterfly's wing the paper was back inside the box, the box shut in the cupboard. The plump maid came in, still wearing her hat, an expression of sheer terror on her face.

'Madame, madame, they're here in the hall. They made me open the door for them.'

'Who are here, Jeanne?'

'The police, Madame. They say you have to go with them. Oh . . .'

Her mouth gaped wide in the beginnings of a howl.

'Well, don't make such a fuss, Jeanne. Go upstairs and fetch me my black hat and the cape with the jet beads.'

Jeanne's feet beat a tattoo up the stairs. Madame Martin glanced at me then very calmly took off her cap and her white apron and folded them on the table. Three men were waiting for her in the hall, one holding a piece of paper. When they told her that she was wanted for further questioning in connection with the murder by poison of Mr Gregory Mordiford she simply said, 'That's foolishness,' in the way you might say it to a troublesome child and made them wait until her hat and cape were adjusted to her satisfaction. By then, Sylvie had appeared white-faced on the stairs.

'What's happening, Mama?'

'I said, foolishness. The mountains are ready. See that they're delivered tomorrow.'

One of the men opened the front door for her and Madame Marie Martin, confectioner and suspected poisoner, was driven away. My fingers were still sticky with her chocolate. I moved to lick it off, paused and thought about it, then licked anyway. It was good chocolate.

ELEVEN

SYLVIE SNAPPED AT THE MAIDS to stop crying and then went running for a lawyer. Seeing that there was nothing I could do I carried my bag to the pension by the station and left it there, wondering how long I'd be able to afford even the modest two francs a night for my bed. Since I could hardly collect my promised fee as interpreter, financial crisis was biting. I should, I suppose, have gone to the Hôtel du Mont Blanc to offer Beatrice my shoulder to cry on, but I knew my shoulder would get restless quite quickly. Beating away in my brain after seeing that piece of paper in Madame Martin's kitchen was the certainty that events of thirty years ago were still dangerous. It was as if the germs of a disease had been frozen into the glacier along with Arthur Mordiford and had come down with him.

I walked to the office of the Compagnie des Guides. It was late afternoon by then and I found it almost deserted, just a young man behind the desk with a ledger and a big piece of rock crystal on it to hold down the page and an old man in a corner whittling an eagle from a block of wood. I told the young man, quite truthfully, that my father had climbed in Chamonix a long time ago and I was interested in talking to some of the guides from the old days.

'There was one called Antoine. I don't know his surname.'

He wrinkled his forehead. We were talking about a time before he was born.

'I could look up the register, but there were probably several Antoines.'

The old man laughed from his corner and said a name that sounded like a bee buzzing.

'Izzydy, that's who you want. Izzydy knows all of them.'

The young man's face cleared.

'Easyday. Yes, Easyday knew them all.'

His smile suggested stories waiting to be told if he weren't on duty.

'The old English lady? I've seen her on the mountain. Where can I find her?'

The old man put his eagle aside, took my arm in a firm grip and walked me to the door.

'That's where Izzydy lives.'

He was pointing towards the lower slopes of the Brevent. Among the trees I could make out the roof of a small chalet.

'Do you need a guide?' He was still chuckling.

I said thank you, but no. Half an hour later I was on my way up the path with my walking breeches in the pack on my back.

It was stubbornly in my mind that if I knew more about what happened on that last climb I might know why Gregory had died. So far I'd had contact of a kind with two members of the party: Gregory who wouldn't talk about it at all and Pierre who'd certainly told me less than he knew. That suspicion had changed to a certainty now he'd disappeared so abruptly. My third source of information, the journal, had raised more questions than it answered and I'd already made one wrong assumption from it. As I walked I tried to revise my mental picture of Arthur Mordiford in the light of what I'd learned.

I'd seen him as a four-square sentimental Victorian, overstepping conventions a little in relations with his fiancée, but I'd been inclined to like the two of them better for that. I liked him less now. To carry on an affair with Marie Martin, under her husband's roof and with his fiancée lodged next door, then to desert her, pregnant with his daughter, were the actions of what his contemporaries would unhesitatingly describe as a cad. I felt angry at the thought of how he'd gone out climbing

90

day after day, depending on Lucien Martin's skills as a guide to keep his smug body safe while all the time he was cuckolding him at home. If Lucien Martin had guessed . . .

I stopped dead in the path. If I'd been Lucien Martin and if I had found out, then I'd have been strongly tempted to take my ice-axe and plant it squarely in the cad's treacherous forehead. I remembered Arthur's body as I'd seen it on the glacier, the gash gaping above the closed eyes. I remembered Lucien Martin's son standing over the body, telling me how Arthur might have done it with his own ice-axe, even miming the action. A red squirrel was staring at me from the stump of a pine tree. I walked on slowly, wondering what I might release from the ice of thirty years ago if I did succeed in finding the other guide, and if I still wanted to do it. The quote in the journal looked different now, as well as most other things. Suppose some time between dinner at the Plan de l'Aiguille and whatever happened at the Grands Mulets rocks Lucien Martin had taken Arthur Mordiford aside and told him that he knew about the affair because his wife had admitted it. It would be typical of Arthur the cad to blame her for that and label her in his journal as a whore. How much would his younger brother know about all this? Quite a lot about the affair, I guessed, but nothing about the rest – if there had been a rest. He would hardly have accepted hospitality from the widow of a man he suspected of killing his brother.

I came to a patch of open pasture with a hut for storing hay, a good place to change from skirt into breeches. It was evening by then with the hut throwing a long shadow and I knew I'd left it late for a walk up the mountain. Even if I did find Easyday, I'd have to come down in darkness. I let myself into the hay-scented gloom, unshouldered my pack and unbuttoned my skirt. There were rustlings further back in the hay that I took to be rats, which was fair enough as it was their home, not mine. I had my boots off and was standing in stockinged feet before I realised it wasn't rats at all. In the darkness of the hut something moved and coughed. It was a sharp little human cough. I spun round, trying to see into the darkness, and could just make out a figure. Apologising to it in English and French I grabbed my breeches and backed hastily towards the door, thinking I'd disturbed some old shepherd.

'Please don't worry. I'm sure there's plenty of room for both of us.'

I stopped, amazed. The figure had spoken in home counties English. The voice was amused, husky and female. She came out of the darkness, small and thin, stepping carefully between piles of hay and watched in silence as I got into my breeches and put my boots back on. Then we went out together into the sunlight.

Her silver hair was tucked into a wispy chignon, her face tanned and lined like the contours on a map. She stood straight and seemed perfectly at ease, but there were chalky rings round her irises and the fingers of her small, leathery hands were crooked with arthritis. She wore a man's tweed jacket and a long corduroy skirt, rubbed smooth in patches, that came right down to the grass, with the toes of good leather boots poking out when she walked. Over her arm she carried a pair of tweed breeches that looked even older than the skirt.

'Silly business, isn't it? I only go down to the town once in a blue moon these days, but I suppose one must respect *les convenances*.'

Her eyes inside their chalky rings were very blue and bright. She looked like a female tramp and talked like a hostess in a Mayfair drawing-room.

'Out for a walk, are you?'

'As a matter of fact, I think I'm looking for you.'

She gave me a sideways look.

'Only think?'

'I'm sorry I don't know your proper name. I'm looking for a woman called "Easyday".'

I said it with some diffidence. She laughed so much that she started coughing again, one clawed hand on her chest, the other held up to me, telling me not to go away.

'You've found her. That's me. My governess would have rapped my knuckles, wouldn't she? I should have said:

92

"I am she." '

Her blue eyes were on me again, waiting.

'I asked at the bureau if there was anybody who might know . . .' I paused, trying to phrase it tactfully for once ' . . . might know some of the older guides.'

'The old relics, you mean? Like me. I knew all of them. Still do, the ones that are still alive.'

She smiled, and from somewhere behind the lined face I had the glimpse of a girl happily shocking her elders.

'What was it you wanted to know? I'll tell you if I can, only I can't stay talking long. I want to get down to the town and back before bedtime.'

I introduced myself.

'Any relation to Charles Bray?'

'My father. You knew him?'

More chuckling and a nod of the head. I decided not to go down that particular road at present.

'I was on holiday here, then I agreed to act as an interpreter for Gregory Mordiford.'

'They say the Widow Martin poisoned him. Did she?'

Her directness made me catch my breath, like finding myself high up suddenly and in thin air. I was amazed too that the town gossip had got up the mountain so quickly.

'I don't know.'

'Were you there when it happened?'

'Yes.'

'Excuse me for a minute.'

She disappeared back into the hay hut. A few minutes later she came out, having changed back from skirt to breeches. Below the breeches were thick peasant stockings in unbleached wool.

'I don't think I need go down to the town after all. We shall go back up together, if you'll be kind enough.'

It was a command rather than a request. She set off up the path at a good pace, apparently with no doubt that I would follow her. I caught up.

'Good. Now tell me about it.'

I decided that it would do no harm, since most of the town seemed to have decided what had happened already.

up through the woods with the light fading
squitoes buzzing I told her a fair part of what I
ew about the death of Gregory Mordiford. Naturally I
left out the affair with Marie Martin, and the written
acknowledgement by Gregory that Sylvie was Arthur's
daughter. She listened in silence, walking steadily all the
time. When I'd finished she rummaged in the pocket of
her breeches and produced a dented flat tin and a box of
matches.

'Cigarette?'

'No, thank you.'

She grinned at me as if I'd been offered a dare and
refused it, produced a cigarette from the tin and lit it
without breaking her stride. It smelt like burning straw but
at least it kept the mosquitoes away.

'So why are you looking for old guides?'

'I want to know what happened thirty years ago when
Arthur died.'

'Why?'

'I think it's connected.'

'I suppose everything is, sooner or later. Did they talk
about it to you much?'

'Very little. His daughter kept talking about a fiancée
who went mad when Arthur died, but that was all.'

She stumbled on a tree root, drew in an extra lungful of
smoke and spluttered to a halt. Alarmed I took her arm
and found it was trembling.

'Oh dear, oh dear, oh dear.'

'Come and sit down. There's a tree trunk over here.'

She shook her head stubbornly and walked on, but the
trembling continued. It was only when she managed to
speak that I realised that she was shaking with laughter.

'Is that what his family are saying? Is that what they've
been saying all this time? Mad with grief?'

'Yes.'

'Mad with grief. For Arthur Mordiford of all people. Oh
dear, oh dear.'

She was, I realised, playing on her audience of one and
enjoying herself immensely. All very well, but it was

getting dark and we were still a long way from anywhere.

'Would you mind telling me what this is all about?'

Instantly, as at the voice of that long-ago governess, she recovered her drawing-room manners.

'I do beg your pardon, Miss Bray. You have a right to be puzzled, but I have a right to be amused. I should have introduced myself properly.'

She stopped and faced me, drawing herself up to her full height and announced with conscious drama, 'I am Daisy Belford, once fiancée to the late Arthur Mordiford.'

I stared. She stared back, still trembling with laughter, drinking in my surprise.

'You think I really am mad, don't you? If I am, I can assure you that it isn't from grieving over poor Arthur. Total nonsense. Come on and I'll tell you about it.'

So she talked, as we walked up together through the woods in the last of the light. She wasn't far into her story before I was convinced that she was sane and telling the truth as she saw it. No impostor could have known so much, and there would have been no point that I could see in the imposture.

'My mother insisted that I should get engaged to Arthur because she said he was my last chance. I had a reputation for being an argumentative gel and that scared men off, so there I was, thirty years old and on my way to being a happy old maid. Well, they couldn't have that, of course not. My family and Arthur's family had business interests in common, so when poor Arthur was finally persuaded to propose to me, I had to accept. I didn't dislike him. He was no worse than any of the other men gels got engaged to. So off we all went for a holiday to Chamonix, Arthur and his brother, two of their university friends, myself and Mama along as chaperone.'

'Where did you stay?'

In this cascade of talk, I tried for a toe-hold of checkable fact. She hardly paused.

'Mama and I were next door to the Martin house. They didn't have room for us with the rest. Anyway, off went the men climbing all day and Mama and I would be left with our sketch books and her embroidery and so it happened, of course. I fell in love.'

Another of her sideways glances at me, the glint of her eye just visible, daring me to be shocked.

'Not, I take it, with your fiancé?'

'Not with poor Arthur, no. Nor any man. Can you guess?'

'Tell me.'

'Mountains.' Pause. 'Do you understand?'

'I think so.'

'I'd never seen mountains before, nothing higher than the Chilterns. As soon as Arthur helped me down from the carriage and I looked up and saw the Aiguilles of Mont Blanc, it hit me here.'

She banged her chest with her small, clawed fist.

'I knew for the first time what I wanted to do with my life. I wanted to climb them, I wanted to live among them, I wanted not to be parted from them for the rest of my life.'

'Did you tell your mother or Arthur?'

'No point. To him you went up 'em, came down 'em and then went home. To her they were just things to sketch, very badly. I was supposed to have my holiday, go home and marry Arthur, and if I behaved like a good little wife and asked politely, he might bring me out to the mountains with him every few years or so. I made up my mind to break off the engagement. Leave it to the last day of the holiday, I thought. Mama was always travel-sick on journeys so she'd be feeling too ill to nag me about it on the way home.'

'But it never came to that.'

'No. When they told me poor Arthur was dead I couldn't help feeling guilty at first, as if I'd wished it, though heaven knows I'd never meant him any harm.'

'His niece thinks you went wandering among the glaciers looking for him.'

This brought on another attack of laughing and coughing.

'Well, she's right that I did walk round the lower bits of

96

some of the glaciers when they were all fussing over mourning clothes and black-edged cards. Only I wasn't looking for Arthur, I was studying ice structures. Fascinating.'

'You never went back to England?'

'No. Mama convinced herself it was grief for Arthur and I suppose I let her think so because it saved arguments. Anyway, after a few months she had to go home and I found myself lodgings with a highly respectable French family. After a while she just had to accept that I was staying here, and that was that.'

'And you had no more contact with Arthur's family?'

'None at all. Mind you, I can see why they'd be glad to let this mad-with-grief story get around. Reflected credit on their Arthur, in a way, and much more respectable than the woman he nearly married scrambling up mountains with guides and foreigners and God knows who.'

The path flattened out and the trees thinned so that we could see the last of the light on the peaks and the electricity coming on in the town below. We arrived at a small terrace with a ramshackle wooden chalet on it and the woods falling away so steeply beneath that it seemed to hang over the valley. A dog barked from somewhere at the back and there was a smell of woodsmoke and kitchen rubbish. She lifted a heavy wooden latch.

'Now you can come in and tell me what's going on down there.'

TWELVE

SHE LIT AN OIL LAMP and its soft light spread round the room, first glinting off dishes and glasses piled on a table, reaching out to the wooden walls with their random collection of shelves at various levels, piled with books, geological specimens and bottles of sinister-looking dun-coloured objects that turned out to be pickled mushrooms. A rope of onions hung down beside half a dozen volumes of Charles Dickens, early editions by the look of them. A pair of snow shoes shared a shelf with an ibex skull, two mouldy peaches and a wood carving of a girl dancing. The light didn't quite reach the far corner where something stirred and rustled in a packing case. A smell hung over it all, part wood, part animal. Easyday opened a small door at the back and shouted to the dog to be quiet, then went over and looked in the packing case.

'What's in there?'

'A baby marmotte. One of the shepherds brought it to me with an injured paw.'

'Will it recover, do you think?'

'Oh yes.'

She had no time for uncertainties. She motioned me to a chair made from a cut-down wine barrel with a sheepskin flung over it and poured two generous measures of red wine into chipped glasses.

'You're not a fool, are you?'

'I hope not.'

'But you've come up here on a wild goose chase over something that happened thirty years ago. Why?'

'There's a woman who'll be on trial for her life. I don't

know whether she killed Gregory Mordiford or not. I want to know.'

'What's that got to do with Arthur? There's more to this than you're telling me.'

The wine was rough, but flavoursome. I sipped it and considered. It was tricky ground because she had been engaged to Arthur after all, even if she didn't love him.

'You must have seen something of Marie Martin, lodging next door.'

She chuckled.

'Mama used to get so angry. She thought a woman who kept a guest-house had no business to be as beautiful as Marie Martin.'

'Did she have any other reason for being angry?'

She gave me a sideways look.

'For goodness' sake, don't talk round things. I never had time for that.'

So I gave it to her straight: 'The night before he died Gregory Mordiford signed a paper acknowledging that Madame Martin's daughter Sylvie was fathered by Arthur Mordiford.'

Her glass almost slipped from her bent fingers. She put it down on the table, staring at me.

'Why in the world did he do that?'

'There's some evidence that Arthur really did have a love affair with a woman in Chamonix. I've seen the journal that was found with his body. There are marks in it that might refer to romantic assignations. When they're camping on their way up Mont Blanc he was thinking about a lighted window in the valley.'

'Not mine, at any rate. We were at the back. You couldn't have seen my light from the Mont Blanc side.'

'No.'

'Besides, he wouldn't have been mooning over a light in my window. What were those marks of yours?'

'Stars against dates. One star at first, then two, then finally three.'

She considered it and puckered her mouth.

'I see. One for a kiss, two for a kiss and a hug, three

99

for . . . hmmm.'

She picked up her glass again, looking at me over the rim of it.

'In his journal, you say. Have you brought it with you?'

'No. Gregory had it sealed in the coffin with Arthur.'

'I'd have liked to see it. They all wrote journals, of course. Very solemn. Anybody would think they were the first people who'd ever gone climbing.'

The self-possession she'd lost for a moment had come back, almost too much for my purposes. I said, as gently as I could: 'So you see, there does seem to be some support for this claim about Sylvie.'

She shook her head, not emphatically but with a calm certainty that I was wrong.

'No, that can't be it. Not Arthur, he really would be the last man in the world. Women scared him. When we got engaged his father had to tell him to kiss me. After that, if he thought he ought to kiss me, he'd ask my permission first then screw up his eyes like this.'

She mimed a timid little peck, like a bird taking seed, then gave me a look that as good as said she'd had more satisfying kisses since.

'Heaven knows what would have happened on our wedding night. Probably just as well he was spared that, poor man. Anyway, whatever your stars stand for they can't be Arthur having a romance with Marie Martin, or any other woman, come to that.'

She topped up our glasses. I felt respect for her obstinate vanity. She might never have loved Arthur, but even thirty years on she wasn't going to let another woman claim him. Even I would never be tactless enough to threaten that vanity by pointing out that a young man disconcerted by an argumentative older fiancée might quite easily fall into Marie Martin's available arms.

'In any case, I don't see how any of this helps Marie Martin, if you are trying to help her.'

'Some of the case against her may turn on this note that Gregory signed. She was desperate enough to ask me if it would still be valid now he's dead. If, as you say, it's not

100

true that Sylvie is Arthur's daughter . . .'

'It isn't.'

'. . . then why did he sign it and promise her two thousand pounds?'

She didn't even try to answer that, so I had to do it myself.

'One thing that occurred to me from the start was that the family knew that Arthur was in some way responsible for her husband's death. Do you think he would have been careless on a mountain?'

'Quite probably. Young men were arrogant in those days. Thought just because they were English the world would roll over on its back for them with its paws in the air. Still do.'

'Did they tell you much about the accident at the time?'

'No. I didn't ask.'

'That was surprising, wasn't it, being interested in mountains as you were?'

'I don't suppose they'd have told me the truth anyway. They always tidy up mountain accidents for the families.'

'But later, when you were living here?'

She shook her head.

'Every summer there are a new lot of fools coming out and getting themselves killed. Why dwell on something that happened a long time ago?'

'Because I think it has links with what's happening now. That's why I was hoping somebody might be able to introduce me to one of the other guides who was with them. There was one in particular called Antoine, small and dark-haired. I don't know his other name.'

'Antoine Bregoli. He's French, but his father was born on the Italian side.'

'Is he still alive?'

'Oh yes.'

'Where does he live?'

'Just down there through the woods. I'll take you to see him tomorrow, if you like. No point now, they go to bed early. You can stay here with me tonight.'

She made supper for us, potatoes boiled in their skins

101

and cheese toasted at the wood fire until it was brown and blistered, washed down by more glasses of red wine. The dog, a German Shepherd, was let in from the yard for its share then sighed and settled down in front of the fire.

'Is it true young Pierre's gone off up the mountain?'

Young Pierre, when he was forty-something. I marvelled at her intelligence network, perched up there on her own.

'Yes.'

'I heard he'd taken his dog and his crossbow with him. Probably stay up there for days.'

'Crossbow?'

'For hunting.'

She wouldn't discuss the Martins and the Mordifords any more that evening but was quite happy to talk about her life in the mountains, once she'd cut loose from England and her family. She knew the Mont Blanc range as well as if she'd been born there, had been up Mont Blanc several times and done a couple of first ascents on other peaks with local guides as her companions.

'Only as a friend, not a client. We had some good times.'

Once, when I called her Miss Belford, she stopped me and said I must call her Easyday like everybody else did.

'Except the ones who called me Easy Daisy.'

Again, in the lamplight, the sidelong glance and glinting eye of a girl kicking over the traces.

'I was the scandal of Chamonix for a while, but in a place like this there's always a new scandal coming along and they got used to me. Some of the English visitors behaved as if I had the plague, but I didn't care about them.'

She laughed, coughed and lit up another of her rank cigarettes. The smell of it mingled with toasted cheese and dog and dried herbs. After a while she asked me something about myself. She was interested in the climbing I'd done, but not concerned in the least about suffragette activities. She was neither for nor against the Vote, it simply meant nothing to her. As she'd been doing exactly what she liked for much of her adult life, I suppose it wasn't surprising.

102

It was late by the time she decided that we should go to bed.

'This is my bed.'

She opened up a tall cupboard on one side of the fire. Inside was a narrow bunk, its side made up of rough boards, with a straw-filled mattress and a blanket.

'And this one's the guest room.'

An exactly similar cupboard and bunk on the other side, except that this one was filled with hay and smelt slightly canine.

'I put Bismarck in there when he was ill. I don't suppose there'll be too many fleas, but if there are they'll be the healthy mountain ones, not like down in the town.'

She found me a blanket and I used my pack as a pillow. After the first few minutes in the hay I could vouch for the healthiness and mountaineering ability of the fleas, but if you could keep your mind off that it was restful lying there with the cupboard doors open, watching the firelight playing on the walls, hearing the dog snoring and the marmotte rustling in its box.

We didn't go to sleep at once but went on talking from one cupboard to another. I persuaded Easyday to tell me more about her climbs, back in the days when a woman who went climbing was an oddity at best, an immodest athlete at worst. There were stories of long days from dawn to moonlight spent on difficult rock faces beside the Mer de Glace, of bivouacs under rocks beside the glaciers, herself the only woman in a group of men. Later, when the fire was low and I was almost falling asleep, the voice from the other cupboard said: 'People keep on at me to go down to the town to live, for the winters at any rate.'

She sounded sleepy and older.

'Will you?'

'No. If they once get me down there I shan't go up again. I tell them, one spring they'll come and find me in here and that will be that. I leave the door open a crack though, every night, after the first snow comes.'

'Why?'

'For Bismarck. He's a young dog, a lot of life in him. If I

103

can't feed him I want him to be able to get out and down to the town.'

Next morning she was up at first light, talking to the dog and stirring up the ashes of the fire. I stayed in the hay, trying not to scratch as that only made things worse, until the smell of coffee wafted round the room. It was strong, bitter coffee, served in chipped mugs from Queen Victoria's coronation. Before the sun was striking the snowfields opposite we were on our way down through the woods to the home of the guide Antoine. It turned out to be as neat as Easyday's was untidy, with rows of onions and salad stuff in terraced plots and hens clucking. Antoine Bregoli was out feeding his hens, a little bent man leaning on a stick. When he saw Easyday he gave a happy shout, came limping towards her at speed and managed, in spite of the stick, to throw his arms round her neck and kiss her on both cheeks. His wife watched sardonically from among the lettuces. Easyday introduced us, with no mention of why I was there, and he led the way inside, calling to his wife to come and make coffee. He saw me looking at his stick and grinned, showing a few surviving teeth like frost-split rocks.

'Stone fall.'

His right leg was misshapen, the foot pointing inwards.

'He was lucky to survive,' Easyday said.

Grey-haired Madame Bregoli made coffee and produced a plateful of home-made biscuits flavoured with pine kernels, keeping a close eye all the time on her husband and Easyday. They spoke French together and I noticed that though Easyday was fluent, she'd kept a relentless English accent. We talked about climbing and the old days and my father, until Easyday decided it was time to come to the point.

'You've heard about this Martin business? Miss Bray here thinks it's something to do with what happened when the other Monsieur Mordiford was killed all that time ago. She wants to ask you some questions about it.'

It was clear that Antoine Bregoli had heard about the arrest of Marie Martin. He wiped coffee from his white

104

moustache and looked serious.

'How's the boy taking it?'

'Gone off.'

He looked even more serious at that.

'What is it you want to know?'

Across his highly polished table, and with Easyday's quick eyes on us, I said I knew that Arthur Mordiford and the guide Lucien Martin had been killed by an avalanche early in the morning close to the Grands Mulets hut. I deliberately didn't include the eye-witness account I'd been given by Pierre because I wanted it from Antoine's point of view.

'You'd spent all night together in the hut. What exactly happened the next morning?'

'As you said, the avalanche took them.'

His brown hands, large for the rest of his body, were placed flat on the table in front of him, like a child's on a school desk.

'Why Lucien and Arthur Mordiford? Were they in front?'

'Yes.'

'With the rest of you behind them?'

He hesitated.

'Yes.'

I knew from Pierre's account that this wasn't true, but could hardly call him a liar under his own roof. Easyday solved the problem for me.

'I think you should tell her what really happened, Antoine, whatever it is.'

He gave her a pleading look.

'You've never asked before.'

'I've never wanted to know before. But Miss Bray thinks it's important and I can see she doesn't believe you.'

He looked down at his hands as if they had the answer. The top of one thumb was just a cap of shiny skin, the nail missing.

'Well then, it was like this . . .'

The start of his story tallied with Pierre's, waking up in the morning to find that it was light already, surprised about it because the party should have been on its way by then. He looked for Lucien Martin to wake him, but couldn't find him.

'His pack was there though, and his rope. I woke up the boy to ask him if he knew where his father was. He didn't know, so the two of us went out together.'

'Only the two of you?'

'Yes. We saw the body of Monsieur Mordiford almost at once. He was lying near a big crevasse. Then we saw Lucien on the slope above him.'

'Trying to get down to him?'

He looked at me, then at Easyday.

'Go on,' she said.

'Yes, I think he might have been trying to get down to him.'

'You say you saw Arthur Mordiford's body. Does that mean he was already dead, before the avalanche hit him?'

'Yes.'

'You were up above him, near the hut?'

'Yes.'

'So how did you know he was dead and not just unconscious?'

His hands moved towards each other and clasped together.

'The blood.'

'What?'

Easyday and I both spoke at once. Her eyes mirrored my shock.

'A lot of blood, from his head, all over the snow. It looked as if somebody had been killing a goat down there.'

'Did Pierre Martin see that as well?'

'He couldn't have helped seeing it. I made him go back to the hut, told him to fetch the other guides, but I couldn't stop him seeing it. He was on his way back when the avalanche started. I shouted out to Lucien, but it was too late.'

'There really was an avalanche?'

'Yes. In Lucien's place, I'd never have tried walking across that slope. He can't have been as cool as he usually was, or he wouldn't have gone that way.'

'And the avalanche took Arthur Mordiford's body into the crevasse?'

'Yes. Probably just as well.'

'Did you tell anybody else what you'd seen?'

'Not until now.'

'So you two were the only people who knew about the blood?'

He nodded.

'That's right. Just me and the boy. Pierre.'

THIRTEEN

EASYDAY AND I LOOKED AT each other and I was sure she understood the significance of that as well as I did. Antoine seemed more disturbed than she was. One of her clawed hands patted him gently on the shoulder.

'Were there tracks down to the crevasse?'

He seemed surprised, but answered immediately.

'Yes. More than one person.'

'So if Lucien had gone down there with him, he probably came up the same way, then started crossing a dangerous snow slope up above him. Can you think why he might do that?'

'No.'

The answer was slower this time. I thought that he, like me, was beginning to see what might have happened. Lucien might have chosen a dangerous slope with the intention of setting off an avalanche to sweep away Arthur Mordiford's body. If so it had worked perfectly, apart from the fact that it had taken Lucien along with it too.

'Can you think of any reason why Lucien Martin might have taken an ice-axe to Arthur Mordiford's head?'

He glanced at Easyday.

'Say it.'

'There was talk . . . about his wife.'

'You thought at the time that Lucien Martin killed Arthur Mordiford because of an affair between him and Marie Martin? Do you still think that?'

He nodded again, very reluctantly. It must have been a blow to Easyday's pride across the years but you wouldn't have guessed it. She said, quite gently, 'You might have told me, Antoine. I should have known what people were saying about it.'

He burst out suddenly, 'I was ashamed for Lucien. He shouldn't have done it. It was a terrible, dishonourable thing to do.'

From a Frenchman with Italian blood, that surprised me.

'But if he thought Arthur Mordiford had abused his hospitality and was carrying on a love affair with his wife . . . ' I began.

Easyday said, 'That wasn't what you meant, was it Antoine?'

She explained to me: 'It's not murder that's worrying Antoine, it's the relationship between a guide and his monsieur.'

Antoine looked at her and nodded. He seemed ashamed of his outburst and trusted her to do the talking for him.

'A guide's responsible for his monsieur's safety, at risk of his own life if necessary. It's the guide's duty to bring him down alive and well.'

'Even in those circumstances?'

'Makes no difference.'

I asked Antoine: 'What would you have done in Lucien's place?'

He found his voice again, and made little chopping motions with his hand on the table to emphasise what he was saying.

'If I knew such a thing I wouldn't be his guide. But if I found out after we started then, as Easyday says, I should bring him down as safely as a mother carrying a baby. Not a hair of his head would I damage.'

I started to say that Lucien apparently hadn't felt the same, but Antoine hadn't finished.

'Then, once off the mountain, once I knew he was quite safe, I would refuse a guide's fee, I would look him in the face and I would . . .'

He mimed unmistakably and with serious expression, the action of hacking an ice-axe into somebody's forehead.

Easyday said, 'But not on the mountain, there's the difference.'

109

It was a long time before any of us spoke. I was thinking about Gregory's last walk up to the glacier, with only his son and nephew and Pierre Martin. Something happened then that shook Gregory worse than anything since he'd returned to Chamonix. Could it have been that he'd built up his own suspicions about his brother's death, put them to Pierre and somehow forced him to confirm them? Now Gregory was dead and Pierre had disappeared. It looked as if Pierre had grown up hiding the knowledge that his father was not only guilty of murder but had broken the code of the mountain guides – something that Antoine seemed to regard as a far worse sin. Would Pierre be capable of doing the same thing to keep the crime secret?

Antoine meanwhile was thinking his own thoughts. His hands were still curled round the shaft of an imaginary ice-axe.

'I'd never have thought it of him,' he said.

'Lucien Martin?'

'I was thinking of the other one, Monsieur Arthur Mordiford. He always seemed a very correct sort of young man.'

That was very much what Easyday had said about Arthur, but it surprised me from Antoine.

'You didn't know him very well, did you? There were only those few days when you were guiding him.'

'And the year before.'

For some reason this worried me, but why shouldn't Arthur Mordiford have come to the Alps for two consecutive summers?

'Yes, he was there with some different friends and his brother wasn't with them. I was one of their guides for a month. He hadn't been up a mountain before. I had to teach him everything.'

'You're quite certain that you climbed with Arthur Mordiford in the summer of 1879?'

'Yes. I'll show you.'

He got up and shuffled out of the room on his stick.

'Antoine's quite right. I remember Arthur had just got back from Chamonix when they started pestering me to get engaged to him. That was the autumn before he died.'

She couldn't see why the fact was so important to me, and neither could I at that point. Antoine returned, carrying with difficulty a thick leather-bound book.

'My guide's book.'

These were important possessions of all the guides. Their clients, or messieurs, would write testimonials in them if pleased, and they could be shown to other prospective clients as proof of competence. Antoine put it on the table and carefully turned over the pages. Each new season was preceded by a page with the year written on it.

'There.'

The year was 1879, the date early September.

M. Antoine Bregoli has accompanied us on some excellent days out, including an ascent to the Col du Géant. I have confidence in recommending him to any party as a careful and conscientious guide. Signed Arthur Mordiford.

A very ordinary recommendation, like thousands more in hundreds of guides' books, but it set my mind spinning like a mill wheel in a flood. The trouble was, it didn't feel as if the mill wheel was connected to anything.

'You taught him?'

'Yes. Naturally you couldn't expect a monsieur to write that he had to be taught. I showed him how to use an ice-axe and a rope, and a little about judging the snow.'

'Was he a good pupil?'

'No worse than others.'

'And he remembered what you taught him when he came out the following year?'

'Enough, yes.'

Easyday was puzzled by my questions and becoming impatient.

'I think I'll go down to the town after all. I'd like to know what's happened to young Pierre.'

We thanked Antoine and his wife, who seemed glad to see the back of Easyday, and set off together down the path.

111

In her town wear of the antique corduroy skirt with random twigs and pine needles caught in its trailing hem, Easyday was something of an event when we got down to Chamonix. Everybody from stall-keepers to elderly gentlemen with the Légion d'Honneur in their buttonholes seemed to know her, called out good mornings and wanted her to stop and talk. All this took time, and as I wanted to hurry on and speak to the Mordifords, I asked where I could meet her later.

'Don't worry, I'll find you when I want you.'

I walked on quickly to the Hôtel du Mont Blanc, one of the grandest in town. When I sent up my name Hector came hurrying down, pale and harassed.

'Beatrice has been asking for you.'

I wasn't going to apologise, though I did feel a little conscience-stricken. We went outside to a row of cane chairs set under a striped awning to face the view. Hector was wearing black suit and tie.

'Beatrice's cousin's supposed to be on her way. Ben dashed off to Paris last night to meet her. Luckily the vicar knew an English lady who was kind enough to move in with Beatrice for a couple of nights.'

As chaperone as well as comforter. Beatrice could not be left alone with her cousin, even in these circumstances.

'How is she?'

'Not well. She keeps dwelling on the Martins.'

He stretched out his legs, staring at his highly polished black shoes.

'Does she know Madame Martin's been arrested?'

'Yes. It doesn't seem to help.'

I knew Hector had been keeping something from me and didn't resent that. It was his family skeleton after all. My problem was whether to tell him what I'd learned from the guide Antoine. Fair exchange.

'I was with Madame Martin in her kitchen when they came to arrest her.'

'Did she say anything?'

'Not then, but just before they came for her she showed me something. A piece of paper, signed by your uncle,

112

witnessed by you, acknowledging that Sylvie was Arthur Mordiford's daughter.'

'Oh God.'

He was still staring at his shoes. I couldn't see his face.

'Is it true?'

'So Uncle said.'

'Why did he sign it?'

'I don't know. On Wednesday night I thought everybody had gone to bed, then I heard a very quiet knock on my door and there was Uncle, still fully dressed. He asked me to come down to the dining-room at once and not ask questions.'

'So you did?'

'I was his company secretary, after all. I went down and there was Madame Martin, sitting in her usual place at the head of the table, cool as an ice-cap. He asked me to sit down, showed me the statement, signed it and asked me to witness it.'

'Did either of them say anything?'

'No.'

'Did you ask anything?'

'He'd told me not to ask questions. Gregory knew his own mind. When he said something, I didn't argue.'

'What did you do after that?'

'Went back to bed – and worried.'

'What about?'

'Mainly the effect it would have on Beatrice if it got out.'

'Why should you be worried about that? After all, she never knew her uncle.'

'No, but she's an idealistic girl, and she's made something of a cult of this wretched fiancée. I think it would hurt her very much if she thought Arthur had been . . . well, you know.'

I wondered if Beatrice's idealism would stand the shock of meeting Easyday.

'It will have to come out at the trial, won't it?'

'Yes, but I hope we'll have Beatrice back in England long before that.'

'Did you tell the examining magistrate?'

'I had to. He wanted to know every detail of Gregory's last day, his state of mind and so on. I didn't like having to do it.'

He raised his head and looked at me miserably. Two children and their nurse walked decorously past us and away down the path between flower-beds, pink ribbons fluttering from their white hats.

'I can't help thinking that's what made them arrest Madame Martin,' he said. 'Motive.'

I thought how anxious she'd been to know if the document would still be valid now Gregory was dead.

'But surely it would go the other way. Her interest was in keeping Gregory alive, so that he'd pay her the two thousand pounds and help her move to Geneva.'

'I've been telling myself that. But suppose he changed his mind on the picnic. He was pretty angry when he caught Ben and Sylvie at the waterfall.'

'Angry enough to tear up the agreement?'

'I don't know. I suspect whatever negotiations went on between Uncle and Madame Martin before I was called in would have included a clause about calling off Sylvie.'

'Calling her off?'

'Part of the pressure on Uncle, don't you think, seeing those two together? Madame Martin's a lady who thinks a long way ahead.'

I waited for an old man in a wheelchair and his attendant to trundle past.

'Do you think Madame Martin poisoned your uncle?'

A long, deep sigh.

'I don't know what to think, and that's the truth.'

We sat in silence for a while and I made a decision.

'What happened when the four of you were up at the glacier?'

'What do you mean?'

'Something gave your uncle a bad shock. Do you know what it was?'

'I'm beginning to have an idea that you do.'

'He was talking to Pierre Martin for some time on his own, wasn't he?'

'Yes.'

'Do you think it was something Pierre told him?'

'I've wondered about that. I don't know. Do you?'

I'd decided that I wouldn't tell him all the details of Antoine's story at present, but the family had a right to know.

'Has it struck you that there's a possibility that your uncle was murdered by Lucien Martin?'

At first he didn't react at all then, very quietly: 'What makes you think that?'

'The motive. If it's true about your uncle and Madame Martin, and he knew it.'

'And you think Gregory knew, or guessed.'

'He might have suspected. I don't think he could have known unless Pierre told him something.'

'But what's that got to do with Uncle's being poisoned?'

'I don't know.'

'And why did Madame Martin have some kind of hold over Gregory? We could all see that. If her husband had killed his brother, surely it should be the other way round.'

That had puzzled me too. I thought the answer might be that she'd made a shrewd calculation about the market value of avoiding family scandal. My own opinion was that Lucien Martin came out of the story more sympathetically than Arthur Mordiford, even if you included murder, but I could hardly say that to one of Arthur's family.

Hector looked at his watch and regretted that he had to leave me. He had an appointment with the vicar at midday. We walked back to the hotel.

'We're burying them both here in the English churchyard, Gregory and Arthur.'

'It seems sensible.'

'Ben's decision, before he dashed off to Paris. I didn't argue. It's a good sign if he's facing up to decisions. There'll have to be a lot of that from now on.'

It hadn't struck me until then what a change Gregory's death had made in his son's status. Two days ago he'd been a rebellious dependant, scolded like a schoolboy and having to plead unsuccessfully with his father for money to be an artist. Now, presumably, he could do what he wanted.

'The firm's his?'

'Oh yes, Gregory was always quite open about his will. There are generous bequests to Beatrice and to me, but of course the son inherits. Poor Gregory thought there'd be at least ten years for Ben to settle down before he had to take over.'

'And if he doesn't settle down?'

'He will. There are good things in Ben, although they may not have been on display much recently.'

The reception desk said Beatrice had gone out for a walk. I found her and her companion at a point where most of the popular promenades meet, a big brass telescope near the river bridge. The companion, a cushiony little lady full of energy and good works, was trying to interest Beatrice in the view through the telescope of climbers going up Mont Blanc, hardly the most appropriate diversion given the family history.

'Oh, do come and look, my dear. They've been stuck there for ever such a long time. I'm sure they're in trouble. No, one of them's moving. Oh.'

An exclamation of annoyance because the telescope's attendant was indicating her time had run out. She fumbled in her bag for change, afraid of missing something. I gave the attendant fifty centimes and suggested to Beatrice that we should walk over the bridge. She seemed pleased to see me in a dazed way, but her eyes were misted with tears and she moved like somebody recovering from a serious illness, weighed down by her black mourning dress.

We stood looking down at the water. Music drifted over from the band playing outside the municipal casino, something by Offenbach.

'It was so unfair, that's what I keep thinking. It was so unfair on him.'

'Your father?'

'Yes. He was only trying to do his best for everybody, for

116

Ben, for me, even for those terrible, terrible women, and all we did was to betray him.'

'I'm sure that's not true. Why should you think you betrayed him?'

'He was worried because I wanted to marry Hector.'

'Had he forbidden it?'

'No, but he'd asked me to wait and I know he'd hoped I'd change my mind and meet somebody else. Then there was all this trouble over Ben.'

'That's not unusual between fathers and sons. I'm sure it would have been all right in time.'

'But he didn't have time, did he? He died before he and Ben had a chance to make their peace. He wanted that, I know he did. He was trying to talk to Ben when he . . . when he . . .'

She was crying, leaning on the bridge rail. I put my arm round her.

'But that means something, doesn't it? Don't you think he'd forgiven Ben and wanted to tell him so?'

She shook her head. I didn't know whether it was disagreement or incomprehension.

'He'd been so angry with Ben because of those wicked women. Do you believe in witches?'

In other circumstances the question would have been funny in its suddenness.

'No, but I believe there are evil people, male and female.'

'More than evil. Real witches . . . spells.' She was hardly coherent. 'You've seen her in the kitchen, all those pans. And the other one, the way she made Ben look at her, though she's hideous, hideous. Those big staring eyes of hers and that long neck like some awful, murderous bird . . . like a heron waiting for goldfish. They still guillotine people in France, don't they?'

Her hand came up and tightened on my wrist. She turned her head and stared at me, really wanting to know.

'Yes.'

'I was dreaming of it last night, that neck stretched out under it like a bird's, like a snake's. And her mother too.'

She stared at me, eyes more than a little mad, as the tourists strolled past and men touched their hats to us.

After a while she was calmer and talked about her brother. He'd been so shocked by their father's death that he'd hardly been able to speak to her. It had been good of him to think of summoning her favourite cousin from England but she wished he hadn't insisted on going to Paris to meet her. She wanted him with her because he was all she had now, apart from Hector. She decided that she wanted to go back to the hotel in case there was a message from him to say when he and the cousin would be arriving, so we detached the companion from the telescope and walked back with her. Beatrice at once went to the reception desk and found there were no messages, but while she was there a boy came in with a telegram.

'Miss Mordiford? Telegram from Paris.'

She grabbed it and ripped open the envelope. It seemed to take her a long time to read it, then she looked up at us and re-read it, frowning. She handed it to me.

'What does it mean?'

It was clear enough as far as it went:

Beatrice, join me immediately in Paris. Will explain. Take evening train if possible, first tomorrow if not. Will meet all trains at terminus. Don't worry about luggage. Do not, repeat do not, tell Hector.

There was a little cry from the English companion and I felt Beatrice's weight slumping against me. We managed to catch her before she fell and got her to a chair, with hotel staff fussing round. Somebody fetched water. A boy was sent running for brandy and smelling salts. When her eyes opened they focused on me.

'What does he mean? What should I do?'

I could hardly have advised her in any case, because at that moment Hector came in with the vicar. When he realised who was in the middle of the confusion he was with us in a bound.

'What's happening? Beatrice, my poor dear, what's happened now?'

He took her hand and rubbed it. She gave him a brave smile and after a few minutes decided that she was well enough to walk to the lift, with his help. The companion started to say something about a shock in the telegram, but Beatrice cut her off.

'Oh no, it wasn't the telegram. That was just from Ben to say he'd arrived safely in Paris. I think I stayed out in the sun too long.'

Which, given that she'd just recovered from an obviously genuine collapse, was quick thinking. It meant that Beatrice, torn between disobeying her brother or deceiving her fiancé had decided, for the moment at least, to give Ben the benefit of the doubt. Also, she had to trust me not to tell Hector there and then. The telegram was still in my hand as I watched the lift doors close on them, with companion and hotel manager in attendance. When I got out into the sunshine I read it again. I could see why it had shocked her. To me it looked very much as if Ben Mordiford had followed the example of Pierre Martin and taken flight.

FOURTEEN

I WAS SITTING ON A bench in the square, wondering what to do next, when I noticed that an elderly gentleman had just strolled past me for the third time in a few minutes. He was an elegant old man in a light suit with a long jacket, a black walking cane and a white goatee beard. The first time he passed I hardly noticed him. The second time it struck me that he was looking at me, and by the third time there was no mistaking his interest. Taking him for a town bore, with stories to tell, I gave him a distancing look. He stopped, took off his hat and gave a formal little bow.

'Please excuse my impertinence, but have I the honour of addressing Miss Nell Bray?'

I told him that he had, heart sinking.

'My intrusion must seem quite unpardonable, but perhaps you would be more inclined to excuse it if I tell you that I am the lawyer to Madame Marie Martin. My name is Louis Veyrat.'

His French, like his appearance, was elegant and formal. He waited, head on one side.

'Then it's no intrusion at all. You want to talk to me?'

'If you have no objection to being seen in public with me, I wonder if you would do me the honour of joining me at lunch.'

After Easyday's cuisine I was ravenous and told him truthfully that I should be delighted. He offered me his arm, I took it and we processed across the square to a café on the corner, watched by no more than several dozen tourists and townspeople.

He waited until we'd disposed of the artichoke hearts

vinaigrette and the first glasses of wine were poured before getting down to business.

'I wonder if you would be kind enough to tell me your version of those sad events, just as you told the examining magistrate.'

Over tournedos Rossini and green beans, I told him as fully as I could, word for word. He listened intently, bending down in his seat occasionally to stroke the proprietor's cat that was nudging round our legs.

'And you witnessed no enmity between Madame Martin and Monsieur Mordiford?'

'None.'

'You saw Madame Martin break the seal of the bottle and pour the Gentian?'

'Yes.'

'But you're convinced that she was nowhere near the mule when the Gentian bottle was broken.'

'Quite convinced.'

I could see his difficulty. In one respect I was a good witness against his client, in another a faint hope for her defence. Dessert arrived, good vanilla ice cream with pieces of ripe peach. He ordered glasses of Muscat wine.

'You've been very courteous, Miss Bray. Might I trespass on that courtesy with an indiscreet question?'

'As indiscreet as you like.'

'Is there anything you didn't say to the examining magistrate that you might be prepared to say to me?'

'Such as what?'

'Such as whether you believe that Marie Martin deliberately murdered by poison her guest Monsieur Gregory Mordiford.'

When I began answering him I listened to myself with some curiosity to know what I was going to say.

'No, I don't think I do. I simply don't understand what her motive would have been.'

'Ah, motive.'

He sucked a piece of ice cream delicately off his spoon and looked sad. My reply hadn't pleased him as much as it should have done.

'Implying that she might have had motives I don't know about?' I asked.

He took a sip of wine as an excuse for not replying. Of course I couldn't expect him to answer that. I decided I'd have to be the one who took the plunge. I was willing to help, but I couldn't do it if we kept waltzing round the question.

'Like the fact that she and Arthur Mordiford were lovers a long time ago?'

I could see from his eyes that this was the reason for buying me lunch.

'Did Gregory Mordiford tell you that?'

'Certainly not.'

'One of his family?'

'No. Madame Martin herself, by implication. There's a paper that was signed the night before he died. Surely you know about it.'

Of course he did.

'Was it your impression that Monsieur Mordiford's family knew about this . . . old friendship, shall we say?'

'I think Gregory may have guessed. His nephew seems to have known about it only when he witnessed the statement. His son and daughter don't seem to have known, either.'

I wondered if I should put to him my theory that Madame Martin's husband had murdered Arthur, and tried the water with another question of my own.

'I suppose you've known Madame Martin for some time. Did it surprise you that she'd had a love affair?'

He gave me a long look and settled back comfortably in his chair.

'I was born here in Chamonix and am, as you see, an old man. In fact, if I may be ungallant about my client, I am of the same generation as Madame Martin. I remember her arriving here as a girl, and like every other young man in the town, I was a little in love with her. I went away to university. When I came back she was married to a guide and had a baby son.'

From the way he was telling it you might have thought

122

he was lost in his memories, but he was watching my reaction all the time.

'I knew Lucien Martin, of course. A handsome man, a dutiful family man, a brave and respected guide. But, strictly between ourselves, a rather boring man. She could have done better. Like the rest of the town I was sorry when he had his unfortunate accident. Perhaps I even had it at the back of my mind that when the young widow finished grieving, she might not have far to look for a new husband. But, as we know, Marie Martin never remarried. Doesn't that strike you as odd, still pretty and such a good head for business too?'

'Perhaps she liked her independence.'

He shook his head.

'Perhaps, but that wasn't the reason. Shall I tell you?'

I nodded. He leaned forward, pursing his lips and whispered across the table, 'The mothers.'

'Um?'

'Men have mothers. I had one myself at the time, and the mothers were unanimous that Marie Martin was not the kind of widow their sons could marry. There were whispers that she might have been perhaps a little too hospitable to the rich and handsome young men who lodged with them. And when her little girl was born, eight months after her husband died, you can be sure that all the mothers bringing sugared almonds to the christening took a good look into the cradle to see if the baby resembled her father.'

'As if they could tell, at that age.'

I felt indignant on Marie's behalf.

'They tell me that women know these things. I wasn't there when the verdict was discussed – but it is a fact that Sylvie Martin was the prettiest young woman in our town, just as her mother was once, and yet she's never married.'

'And the examining magistrate will have heard these old rumours?'

'Oh, he'll know. He's a good man on the whole and will have tried to put them out of his mind, but these things have an influence. So when Madame Martin told him about the paper that Monsieur Gregory had signed . . .'

'She told him that herself?'

At least Hector needn't have felt guilty.

'Yes indeed. I might not have advised it, but that's what she did. She's determined, come what may, that her daughter should have what she thinks is due to her from the Mordiford family.'

I decided I wouldn't tell him about the murder theory, at least not at present. It seemed more likely to make things worse than to help. We finished our ice cream and he said something to the waitress that I didn't hear. I asked him if he thought he would have a strong case for the defence. Quite strong, he said, but his face told me something else. The man who would have liked to marry the pretty widow so long ago was desperately worried about her now, grasping at straws. Coffee arrived, and with it two small glasses full of a pale liqueur.

'Gentian,' he said.

I hadn't needed to be told. The smell rose round us. I could feel necks craning round the café.

'Not Madame Martin's as it happens. You know, there have been some regrettable accidents with this drink.'

'Accidents?'

'Yes. As you know, it is made from the roots of the yellow gentian, a good harmless plant. But there is a plant that grows on the mountains that looks very much the same before the flower comes and is not harmless at all. Veratrum album, the white hellebore. It's a very poisonous plant indeed. There are cases on record of people dying because the two plants were confused by the makers of Gentian. Your health.'

We sipped. Over the glass his eyes were testing the effect his words were having, a trial run for the trial itself.

'That's a possible defence, then, that there was poison in the drink but that it got there accidentally?'

'It's possible, don't you think?'

It's not good to kill hopes, however forlorn, but I had to mention it.

'Beatrice Mordiford had *tue-loup* in her flower

collection. She's convinced somebody took it and I'm afraid she's almost obsessive on the subject of Madame Martin and Sylvie.'

I could see that came as bad news to him. Sooner or later Beatrice would be considered well enough to be interviewed by the examining magistrate.

'It's possible she's mistaken. I've heard – forgive me – that she's an emotional young woman.'

I couldn't disagree. I asked him if he'd talked to Sylvie about his theory that the Gentian might have been poisoned by accident.

'Yes, I've talked to her.'

The depression he'd managed to keep out of his voice so far had seeped into it.

'Sylvie Martin is quite adamant that it's out of the question. She insists that neither she nor her mother could possibly have confused yellow gentian and white hellebore. It seems to be a matter of professional pride with her.'

'Pride can be expensive.'

It sounded to me that if Sylvie had actually wanted to sabotage her mother's defence, she could hardly be doing better. We finished our coffee. I asked him if he thought I should call on Sylvie Martin.

'It might be a kindness. She's very much on her own.'

I noticed that there was less warmth in his voice when he talked about Sylvie rather than her mother. He came part of the way with me and pointed out his office and his flat above it.

'If anything should occur to you, anything at all, I should be most grateful if you'd let me know.'

When we were within sight of the church he thanked me, raised his hat and walked briskly away.

Now that it was deprived of Madame Martin's energy, the house had a look of defeat about it. The shutters on the upper floors were closed and geraniums drooped unwatered in the window-boxes. The plump maid opened the door to me, her apron dirty, her eyes pink and puffy.

'Would you be kind enough to ask Mademoiselle Martin if she'll see me?'

125

She went upstairs, came down and asked me to follow her. Sylvie was sitting at the foot of the big table in the dining-room. The shutters were partly closed and only a dim light filtered through. Sylvie's white dress seemed the brightest and freshest thing in the house. In a low voice she thanked me for coming and invited me to sit down. Now that I was here I didn't know how to start. You can hardly offer conventional sympathies to a woman whose mother is in prison, charged with murder.

'Have you been to see your mother?'

'She sent a message by our lawyer that I shouldn't try to see her.'

'Monsieur Veyrat? I've just been talking to him.'

She nodded and the inclination of her slim white neck reminded me of Beatrice's comparison to a predatory heron. A beautiful neck, even so.

'Monsieur Veyrat thinks poison might have got into the Gentian accidentally,' I said.

'Yes, he came to see me. He seemed quite excited about it, poor old man.'

'He thinks it would be quite easy to confuse the roots of yellow gentian and white hellebore.'

'If you're a fool, yes.'

'Only if you're a fool?'

'Of course. If you know anything about plants the shapes of the roots are quite different. And when you cut into the root of white hellebore the smell is like this, phew.'

She waved a white hand delicately in front of her nose.

'So your mother wouldn't have confused them?'

'I assure you, if Monsieur Veyrat thinks my mother's life depends on making the examining magistrate believe that, then I shall be wearing black.'

She looked at me and ran her fingers down the front of her white dress.

'Did your mother poison Gregory Mordiford?'

'No. Why should she?'

'Do you know who did?'

'No. Do you?'

She asked in a challenging way that stopped just short of

the outright rudeness I'd probably deserved.

'I don't.'

'Why are you interested?'

'Perhaps because I respect your mother.'

'But you're a friend of the Mordiford family.'

'I've only known them for a few days.'

'Are they pleased that my mother has been arrested?'

I said nothing. It wouldn't help Sylvie to know that Beatrice was imagining her neck and her mother's under the guillotine blade. She answered for me.

'Of course they are. It must be very convenient for them. Monsieur Mordiford agrees at last to pay my mother what his family owes her, then suddenly she's in prison.'

'And Mr Mordiford's dead. It would be a drastic way of avoiding paying two thousand pounds.'

She looked unconvinced. I asked her if she believed that Gregory's death and the agreement to pay the money were connected in some way.

'You should ask the family that.'

'Any one of the family in particular?'

She smiled but said nothing. I changed tack.

'Why was Gregory Mordiford so very annoyed when he saw Ben with you at the waterfall?'

I'd expected another of her enigmatic smiles and was amazed to see her blushing. Her flirtation with Ben had seemed quite open and unblushing until then.

'Was there some kind of agreement, that your mother would get the money on condition that you and Ben were no longer friendly?'

'Something like that.'

For the first time she turned her head aside and wouldn't look me in the eye. On an impulse I asked, 'Do you know Ben Mordiford's gone off to Paris?'

I expected to surprise her. All I got was another of her graceful nods.

'How did you know?'

'He came to see me, just before he went to the station. He had a question to ask me that he said I must answer

127

before he left.'

'What was the question?'

Having led me on to ask, she refused to answer. She resented, I think, being made to lose her poise even for a moment and was determined to demonstrate that it was back.

'That is a matter between myself and Mr Mordiford.' Then, with a ghost of a smile, 'But I shall, if you wish, tell you my answer.'

'And what was your answer?'

'My answer to Mr Mordiford's question was yes.'

I recognised that I'd come up against a rock face, however flowery the surface of it. I thanked her, told me where she could find me and stood up. She showed me out herself, very politely, so as not to bother the maids. As the door closed behind me I was still wondering what Ben Mordiford's question to her had been. Could he possibly have proposed marriage? I hoped not.

FIFTEEN

I WENT LOOKING FOR EASYDAY all over the town. In the end I asked at the Bureau des Guides where the man on duty smiled and handed me a note in only just legible handwriting on grubby paper.

Dear Miss Bray,
   I've gone home. Had enough of the town and the marmotte will need feeding. I hope I shall have the pleasure of your company again tonight. Please bring some more wine up with you, also these potatoes.

There were three or four kilos of them, crusted with earth, in a straw bag in the corner of the bureau. Grinning, the guide helped me stow them in my pack. I bought two bottles of red wine and a tin of flea powder at the grocer's and walked up through the hot afternoon to Easyday's cabin in the woods. She seemed pleased to see me and set me to work bringing water in buckets from a stream that threw itself down the mountain about a quarter of a mile away. She complained that I'd used most of a normal day's supply to wash in that morning, a habit she clearly thought unnecessary. When the old barrel she used as a reservoir was full to brimming and a bottle of wine had been opened she condescended to tell me her news.

'Some of the other guides saw Pierre yesterday afternoon going along the Blaitière path.' She gestured to the slopes facing us, below the sharp points of the Chamonix Aiguilles. 'He could live off hare and rock partridge up there for days on end if he wants to.'

'Don't you think it's odd, going off at this time?'

'He was always a bit of a solitary, even as a young man. Of course, after what Antoine told us yesterday you can see why.'

'Even so, his mother's under arrest and his sister's alone in that big house.'

'Not much love lost there. The gossip in the town is that Pierre's a dutiful son, but the mother and sister are much closer.'

'What does town gossip say about Gregory?'

'That she probably poisoned him and her daughter's lucky not to be in prison as an accomplice.'

'Do I gather they're not much liked?'

'Oh, I wouldn't go that far. But they have tended to keep themselves to themselves, and of course Marie Martin was an outsider, not born here. She's done well for herself with the chocolate business, so there's some envy around.'

'Was there gossip about her when you first lived here?'

'Yes, but you can't be as beautiful as Marie Martin was in a place like this and not be gossiped about. Goodness knows, they even gossiped about me for a winter or two, until the novelty wore off.'

'Even if Pierre isn't particularly fond of his mother, surely he shouldn't have gone off like this. You say he's a dutiful son.'

'Perhaps that's why he's gone off – to think about which way his duty lies.'

'You mean he knows something that wouldn't help his mother?'

'It's possible, isn't it? You told me he picked Gregory up in his arms and carried him down the mountain. Perhaps Gregory said something and he was the only one who heard it.'

'Last words, incriminating somebody?'

'The examining magistrate's no fool. The same idea must have occurred to him.'

'That would mean it had happened to Pierre twice. He's spent all his adult life hiding something to save his father's reputation, now you think he may be doing the same thing for his mother.'

'Or his sister. You sound angry.'

'It doesn't seem fair on a man.'

'Oh-ho.'

She looked at me over her glass and laughed.

'Oh-ho what?'

'Fallen for Pierre Martin, have we?'

'We have done nothing of the kind.'

She took no notice.

'Well, you could do worse. He would have been too serious for my taste, but he knows the mountains better than any man in Chamonix.'

To change the subject, I asked if she'd brought any more news from town with her.

'There was one thing that might interest you, though goodness knows what you'll make of it. I was talking to old one-eyed Jacques, you know, keeps the tobacco kiosk. His sister is married to one of the men who hires out mules. It was his mules they were using on the picnic when Gregory died.'

She seemed to be on the point of offering me a four-hooved witness. Dozy from the warm evening and the wine, I tried to concentrate.

'His eldest son, that is old Jacques' nephew, is a bit on the simple side. Nice lad, but has the mind of a child still. Anyway, he's good with the mules and he was leading one of them on your picnic. A baggage mule it was, with a nick out of its left ear.'

'I remember. It kept trying to bite people.'

'Anyway, the lad's name is Nico. His uncle says since Gregory died Nico's been behaving oddly, won't eat, doesn't want to get out of bed, keeps crying and hugging his mother. He won't tell anybody what's wrong. His mother's nearly mad with worry and doesn't know what to do about it.'

'Well, it would be upsetting for any child. I don't think the mule-boys saw the worst of it, but he'd still know what was going on.'

'His mother thinks it's something worse than that.'

'Have they said anything to anybody outside the family?'

'No. His mother's terrified that if word gets out the poor boy will be called in front of the examining magistrate. She says if that happened he'd go mad with fright.'

We began washing the potatoes for supper in a few precious inches of water.

'Would Nico's mother talk to me, do you think?'

'You could try. She's a friendly enough woman when she isn't being driven out of her mind by the children.'

Over dinner, which was exactly the same meal as the night before, I told her about my conversation with Beatrice Mordiford.

'It sounds as if the poor gel needs taking out of herself. You should have brought her up here with you.'

It had crossed my mind, but I'd decided the shock might be too much for her.

'Later on, perhaps. Did I tell you she's written a poem about you?'

Her snort of laughter woke up the snoring dog.

When the plates had been wiped and put on the shelf and we were finishing our wine in front of the log fire, I started on the subject that was worrying me most.

'How reliable would you say Antoine Bregoli's memory would be?'

'You're thinking of Arthur's blood on the snow?'

'No, anybody would remember that. I was thinking of something much more commonplace.'

'To do with climbing?'

'Yes.'

'In that case, his memory's as reliable as the ground we stand on. I've heard him describe a climb that happened forty years ago, every pitch, every crack in the rock, as if he'd done it yesterday.'

'What about the people he climbed with?'

'The same. If he climbed with somebody, he'd never forget them. You heard that this morning.'

'Yes. He was quite sure he taught Arthur to use an ice-axe in the summer of 1879, the year before he died. Can we rely on that?'

'Yes, if it matters. When Arthur was courting me, if you

132

could call it that, he told me about his climbing holiday. I remember I insisted he should bring his ice-axe into the drawing-room to show it to me over tea. His mother thought it wasn't quite nice.'

'So both you and Antoine Bregoli are witnesses that Arthur Mordiford possessed an ice-axe and knew how to use it in 1879?'

'Positive.' She peered at my face in the firelight. 'Why are you looking so worried about it?'

'That means the journal's a forgery.'

'Arthur's?'

'It must be. I'm sure I remember that right at the start of it he was buying an ice-axe and learning how to use it.'

From her face, she'd caught some of my worry.

'Arthur didn't need to buy an ice-axe. He'd brought his out with him. I remember the fuss he made over it at Victoria Station.'

'So he can't have written that journal. But I saw it picked out of the glacier. I assumed it had come down with his body.'

Pierre had been there. An easy enough matter for him to drop a small package where somebody else would find it.

'But how could the Martins have done it?' I asked myself and her. 'One of them would have to write perfect English, quote Dr Johnson. And Gregory read it. If it was a forgery, it would have to be good enough to deceive Arthur's own brother. I just don't believe it.'

'Make up your mind. Either it's a forgery or it isn't.'

'I don't see how it can have been. It must have been authentic and it did come down the glacier with Arthur's body.'

'So?'

The fire crackled. The dog twitched. I thought it through several times before I answered and came to the same conclusion every time.

'It wasn't forged, but it couldn't have been written by Arthur. There were all five names on the first page. The only explanation is that it belonged to one of the other

Englishmen in the party and it was somehow in Arthur's possession when he was swept into the crevasse. Oh, I'm a fool, a fool, a fool.'

I got up and started pacing a square in Easyday's cluttered cabin. I didn't know I was doing it until I hit my shin on a low table.

'I stood there. I stood there and watched him seal it in the coffin. Of course he did. Thank goodness I wasn't the only one to read it. Hector Tenby read it too, only he hadn't met you or Antoine so he wouldn't see the significance of the ice-axe.'

'Would you mind sitting down and explaining? I'm getting a crick in the neck from looking at you.'

I sat.

'There were four Englishmen in that party, Arthur and Gregory Mordiford and two friends called Tom and Ted, I think.'

'Something like that. They were very forgettable young men.'

'I'm pretty sure that both Tom and Ted are mentioned in the journal. I wish I could check that. If so, that should mean that neither Tom nor Ted wrote it. We know Arthur himself didn't write it because of the ice-axe, so that leaves . . .'

We looked at each other.

'No wonder he was in such a hurry to seal it in the coffin. Arthur must have got hold of it somehow from Gregory. So those asterisks . . .'

I stopped short. Easyday gave me a look.

'What is it now?'

'Let's suppose it was Gregory and not Arthur who wrote the journal. If I'd read it knowing that you were with them as Arthur's fiancée I think I'd have assumed . . .'

'That Gregory had been getting up to what he shouldn't with me?'

She was quite unruffled.

'You'd have been wrong, not that he didn't try. He put his hand on my breast once when he was pretending to help me off my mule. Of course, I reacted the way any well

134

brought-up gel would.'

'How was that?'

'Caught him where it mattered with my knee then stood on his foot. You should have heard him gasp. I don't suppose he put any stars in his journal that day.'

The landscape had been turned upside down and I was trying to pick out bits that I could still recognise.

'So we've agreed that the asterisks and the lighted window in the valley definitely weren't you?'

'No.'

'And if the journal isn't Arthur's, there's no proof that he was having a love affair with Marie Martin, apart from that piece of paper that Gregory signed. But Gregory must have been pretty well convinced of it all the same, otherwise why should he . . .'

I stopped, knowing where that was leading, trying to make every step as sure as I could. I had to revise my ideas of what had happened on the last day and a half of Arthur's life. They'd made their evening camp. Gregory had written in his journal about a certain window in the valley. Somehow that journal had come into possession of his elder brother. At some point one of the two of them, either Arthur or Gregory, had written the whore quote. The journal was in Arthur's possession when the avalanche caught him, only Lucien had caught him first. I must have made some sound because Easyday asked me what the trouble was.

'It changes everything, not just then, what's happening now. Oh I wish I had that journal back. How could I be fool enough to stand there and let him seal it up?'

'We could go and get it if you really want it.'

'But it's in his coffin, Easyday. You're surely not suggesting . . .'

'Why not? If you need it, we'll go and get it.'

She said it as casually as if we were talking about buying more potatoes.

'You think about it. We could do it tomorrow night, if you like. I'm going to bed.'

The fleas in my cupboard seemed to like the flea

powder and were at least as bad as the night before, but it wasn't their efforts that kept me awake until daylight washed in over the debris of dog-chewed bones, empty bottles and the unwashed potato pan. I was still trying to get my bearings in that changed landscape.

SIXTEEN

BREAKFAST WAS LARGE CUPS OF coffee again, warmed up by Easyday and as bitter as failed campaigns. It was strong enough to take the varnish off tables, not that there was much left on Easyday's. She said she made two big jugfuls on Sundays and reheated it as needed. No mention was made of the coffin-robbing proposal but I caught her looking at me several times with an expression I'd come to recognise. She'd issued a dare and was waiting to see if it would be accepted. When we'd finished coffee I got ready to go back down to the town.

'I suppose you're going to talk to young Nico. You can bring some more wine up with you if you like, and some peaches.'

It was quite early when I got to Chamonix with most of the visitors still at breakfast in their hotels. There was little risk of seeing Hector or Beatrice up and about so early and I was glad of that. I had things to do before I spoke to any member of the family.

I followed the directions Easyday had given me to the muleteer's house. It was about half a mile out of town on the road down the valley towards les Houches. A broken-down sort of place, she said, off the road and not far from the river. I found it without difficulty, an old stone farmhouse sprawling in the morning sun with a collection of barns round it, sagging at various angles. Several raw-boned mares with pregnant bellies grazed in the field in front of it and two small boys were fighting with each other in the pot-holed drive. They stopped when they saw me, said good morning quite politely and started again as soon as I'd gone past. There were more children in the farm-yard and a scattering of kittens, ducks and bronze-feathered hens. I asked the children if their mother was in and they pointed to a door of sun-bleached planks.

I knocked. From inside, a harassed woman's voice told me to stop playing with the kittens and go and see to the goats. I walked in.

'I'm very sorry to intrude. Are you by any chance Nico's mother?'

She was kneading dough on a big wooden table, an infant crawling at her feet on the stone-flagged floor. She was a plump, red-faced woman with uncorseted breasts pushing out her print dress, a crocheted shawl round her shoulders. The kitchen smelt of milk and yeast.

'Has something happened to him?'

Her hands went on kneading but her face was full of worry.

'Nothing. I'm sorry, I didn't mean to scare you.'

I introduced myself, explained that I was staying with Easyday and that I'd been up the mountain with my friends, the Mordifords, when the event we all knew about happened.

'Easyday says Nico was there,' I said.

'Of course he was there. He was with the mules, like he always is. He's a good boy.'

She wasn't combative, just anxious and distressed.

'I'm sure he is. Any boy would be disturbed by what happened.'

'It's not the old man dying, I'm sure of that. After all, what's an old Englishman to poor Nico?'

'Just so. Then something must have happened to upset him, apart from the old man dying.'

'He won't tell me. He wasn't so bad the first night after it happened. But the next evening Jules comes home and says the whole town is full of Madame Martin being arrested for poisoning the old man for his money with her Gentian. We're all round the table having our soup and Nico jumps up, face as white as skimmed milk, and rushes out to the barn. I bring him in and put him in our bed, like I do when he gets worried about something, then next morning he doesn't want to get up, just lies there under the blanket saying he's going to die and it's his fault.'

'His fault?'

'I ask him what he means but he won't tell me, only starts crying and shivering. Since then he won't eat, won't drink, just curls up in a corner like an old sick dog. Until this morning.'

'What happened this morning?'

'Nico comes to me and says he must go to the town. He's weak from not eating and he can't stop crying. I say stay here with me, but he's set on it and I've got the others to look after and what can I do?'

She patted and rolled the dough into a sausage shape and began slicing it into thick sections without looking at it.

'I could go and look for him, if you like.'

'Why would you do that?'

'Perhaps I could set his mind at rest about whatever's bothering him.'

She seemed a little suspicious, which wasn't surprising, but manacled as she was to her children she needed help.

'If you find him, tell him to come straight home to me.'

'How will I recognise him?'

'He's a big lad, tall as you are. Yellow hair like his father's but long and floppy on account of he'll never sit still long enough for me to cut it. Blue trousers and tunic and his own way of walking – slaps his feet down like our old gander in the mud.'

I thanked her and walked back to the town. The sun was well over the mountains now and the day was hot, with a few cigar-shaped clouds floating above the peaks. As I passed the Hôtel du Mont Blanc I saw the black figure of Beatrice strolling dispiritedly in the garden with the English companion. She didn't see me, but at least one question was answered. So far she hadn't responded to her brother's appeal to join him in Paris. I walked round looking for boys answering to Nico's description. Mule trains were winding their way along the streets on their

139

way to cafés and viewpoints, loaded with tourists, telescopes and picnic hampers. I asked some of the mule-boys if they'd seen him but none had. I strolled on towards the church. There were fewer people in this part of town and none looking like Nico. Then I saw a figure in the shadow of the church wall. He was leaning against the stone, his forehead on his bent arm, shoulders heaving and fair hair flopping down. As I walked towards him he straightened up, shook himself and made purposefully for the church door with exactly the gait his mother had described.

I followed him into the cool, wax-scented darkness and watched as he stood for a long time in front of a saint's statue with a few candles burning. He lit no candle himself, probably having no money to put in the box, but sank clumsily to his knees, head bowed almost to the floor. Minutes of this, then he heaved himself up and, with his determined gander-like walk, made for the tall wooden box of the confessional in a side aisle. He drew aside the curtain and plunged in as if afraid he might change his mind. No place for me. I went out and waited in the sun. It was some time before he emerged and although he seemed calmer he was crying, great washes of tears running unashamedly down his plump but pale cheeks.

'Nico.'

He turned, far too miserable to run away.

'What's wrong?'

'I'm going to die.'

He said it flatly, in a drawling kind of voice, as if the words had to drag themselves out from a cave.

'Come and sit over here and tell me.'

He let me lead him to a bench in the shade. Either his simplicity or his misery had deprived him of barriers against strangers.

'Now, why do you think you're going to die?'

'Because she put poison in the drink.'

He stared at me, his tear-washed eyes very blue.

'Who did?'

'The old woman, Madame Martin. But it's my fault too.

I did something wrong.'

'What did you do that was wrong?'

Surely this was the least likely of accomplices.

'I drank it. I drank the drink with the poison, so I'm going to die. That's why I had to come to confession because I'm . . .'

'But you didn't drink it. It was Mr Mordiford, the old man, who drank it.'

I thought this was simple fantasy. The mule-boys hadn't been invited to the picnic.

'He was the only one who drank,' I said, 'then the bottle got broken when they were loading it on the mule.'

He shook his head.

'Before it got broken they put it down on the ground. One of the other mule-boys picked it up while you were all talking. We didn't know there was poison in it, not then.'

I thought back to the picnic. It was true that the bottle had been put down after Gregory had his drink from it, true also that we'd been too occupied with Gregory to worry about what the mule-boys were doing.

'What happened to the other boy?'

'He took the top off and drank. He made a funny face but he said it was good, very sweet like sugar, then he gave the bottle to me and told me to drink.'

'You did?'

'Yes, I drank a lot of it, a big mouthful like you do with buttermilk when you're thirsty. Only it wasn't sweet at all. It was bitter, like medicine.'

True again. The thing about Gentian was its bitter taste.

'I spat some of it out but I swallowed some. I started coughing and the other boys took me away and put my head in a bush.'

'Why did they do that?'

'If the ladies and gentlemen heard me coughing they'd know we'd been drinking their drink and be angry with us. But oh it was so bitter, so bitter.'

'So there you were, coughing with your head in a bush. I don't suppose you saw what happened to the bottle after that.'

141

He shook his head.

'One of the other boys took it from me.'

And put it in the basket then somebody made a mess of trying to load it on to a mule. There was nothing in Nico's story that contradicted what I knew – apart from the shattering fact that he'd apparently drunk from a bottle containing poison and survived. Although I knew little about the effects of either white hellebore or aconite, I didn't believe that a poison that had killed Gregory so quickly would have left the boy alive days later.

'The other boy who drank, is he ill?'

'No. I saw him going up the mountain this morning with their mules. But he only drank a little drop. I drank more.'

He began crying again, his big body as slack as a toy.

'Are you quite sure you drank from the same bottle as the old man?'

'Yes, the same, the one with the poison.'

'And what was this wrong thing you say you did?'

He stared at me.

'I told you, I drank it. It belonged to the ladies and gentlemen and I drank it.'

'That was all you did?'

His open stare was my answer. He hardly understood the question. I took his hand and gave him stare for stare, willing him to believe me.

'Listen, Nico, are you sure that everything you've told me is true?'

'As true as I told it to the priest in there.'

'Well, I'm telling you the truth as well, and you must believe me. There was no poison in that bottle, Nico, none at all.'

'But it was so bitter.'

'That's the Gentian, not the poison. The other boy was playing a joke on you when he said it was sweet. He's not going to die and neither are you.'

His mouth was gaping and I didn't blame him. My mind was going round in circles too.

'You understand? No poison. You're not going to die.'

'But the old gentleman . . .'

'He died of something else. It can't have been in the Gentian.'

It took a long time to convince him, but in the end I managed it. Then I walked back down the valley road with him until we came to the turning for his farmhouse.

'Your mother will be pleased to see you.'

'Are you going to tell her?'

'About drinking the Gentian? Certainly not. Why don't you just go to her and tell her that you're feeling better now? That will make her happy.'

He beamed, caught me by surprise with a warm, hay-smelling hug then gandered off down the drive, faster and faster as he got nearer his mother. One satisfied client at least, but a whole new spiral of problems for me. I went back slowly along the valley road, thinking hard. Then instead of going into the town I turned up the tourist path towards the Glacier des Bossons, on the route our party had taken the day Gregory died. Going on my own, without luggage and mules, it didn't take me long to get to our picnic place.

Our traces were still there, mule droppings on the path, even the shard or two of a broken bottle, but I wasn't concerned with those. The area where the picnic had been spread showed as a circle of flattened grass. A little further away from it, nearer the ice, were two much smaller, more regular circles where the bright grass was blackened. Beatrice's hot kettle and teapot had rested there. Six paces away, in an area of bare soil under a rock, I found what I'd been looking for and although I expected to find it, it still took my breath away. No blame to the French police if they'd searched and not found it. They didn't know what I knew and in any case it looked so innocent. I went back to the path and found a piece of stick to mark exactly where it had been lying under the rock then wrapped it in a handkerchief and put it in my pocket. I skidded back down the woodland path, dodging tourists around the crowded chalet at the Cascade du Dard. By the time I reached town I'd made my decision. I went to the office of the lawyer Louis Veyrat, gave my name to the clerk and was shown into his office at once. A large flora was open on his desk, so he was still grappling with the unpromising defence of accidental poisoning. At least I could give him something better than that now.

First I told him about Nico. He listened, eyes bright, and made me go through it again while he took notes.

'The examining magistrate will have to know about this.'

'Yes, but don't let him frighten poor Nico, will you?'

'Then there's the other boy who drank. It shouldn't be difficult to trace him. It begins to look as if the poison wasn't in the Gentian. But . . .'

He sighed.

'But what?'

'After all, the man was poisoned. They've sent the organs to Lyons for analysis, but from the symptoms there seems no doubt about it.'

'Could they send something else to Lyons for analysis?'

I brought out from my pocket the object I'd found behind the rock, a little makeshift pouch made from a piece torn off a linen handkerchief, white at the top, where the fabric was gathered together, otherwise stained greenish brown, with no more than a couple of teaspoonfuls of a substance inside it that felt like small crushed leaves.

'I've just picked that up from behind a rock where we picnicked. I'll swear to that if they like, but we need it analysed. If I'm right about what's in it . . .'

'*Tue-loup*?' He seemed reluctant to take it.

'Let's wait for the analyst's report. It looks pretty clear though that whatever it was must have been held in hot water.'

I put it down on the blotter in front of him.

'In the tea? But you said you drank the tea too.'

'I did. That's why we need that analysed.'

He looked at it for a long time.

'If it was in the tea and not in the Gentian, then there's no more evidence against her than against anyone. Except for that statement Gregory signed.'

'Suppose it could be proved that the statement were untrue?'

144

'Why do you ask that?'

'Would you answer my question, please?'

'If Monsieur Mordiford signed an untrue statement at Madame Martin's insistence, that would make things worse for her.'

'But what if it had been to Gregory Mordiford's advantage to lie?'

'You know of something?'

He almost jumped across the desk at me.

'Not yet. But if I did?'

'It would depend on the nature of the lie and his motive in lying. If you know of any such thing, then it's your duty to tell me.' He added reluctantly, 'Or the examining magistrate.'

It was tempting. I could pass over to the authorities the burden of what I almost knew. But if they didn't believe me – and I couldn't blame them for not believing – the chance of proving it might be gone for good.

'As soon as I can prove something that might be helpful, I'll come back to you.'

Monsieur Veyrat didn't like that. When I thought of what it involved, I didn't like it either. I bought peaches, wine and a large screwdriver and walked up through the woods to Easyday.

SEVENTEEN

'WE'LL NEED THIS AS WELL.'

Easyday hissed this at me as we were walking along the narrow street towards the undertaker's. She needn't have bothered to hiss it since it was one o'clock in the morning and the artisans who lived over the small workshops along the street would have been asleep for hours. She was entering into the spirit of the thing all too thoroughly for my liking and had amused herself hooting back at the owls on our moonlit walk down from her cabin. From decades back in her past she'd unearthed a long black cloak with a hood which she'd decided was *de rigueur* for coffin-robbing. I was beginning to think that the fairly eligible young men of thirty years back had a lucky escape when Daisy decided to fall in love with mountains instead. She was offering me the wooden shafted knife she used for carving some of the more obviously rotten bits out of potatoes.

'I hope not.'

'I've brought some candles. They'll do for heating it.'

'Why should we need to heat the potato knife?'

She made an annoyed sound. 'For sliding under wax seals, of course. Don't they teach gels anything useful these days?'

I passed over this slur on Somerville in silence.

'When I was a gel we used to open the grown-ups' sealed letters with a hot knife. If you did it properly you could put the seal back on afterwards and nobody would know it had been disturbed, if they didn't look too closely.'

'I suppose you learned that from your governess.'

146

I'd intended sarcasm, but the black hood nodded and let out a chuckle.

'Yes. She wanted to know what Mama was saying about her in a reference. Did her no good, of course. Dismissed without a character and served her right. Still, at least she taught me something I remember, which is more than all the rest did.'

I could see the *Pompes Funèbres* sign ahead of us. I didn't like this at all, but still couldn't see any other way of proving what had to be proved. Also I should never hear the last of it from Easyday if I backed out now. He had been her fiancé, after all. If she didn't mind this, neither should I.

'I hope he hasn't got an apprentice sleeping under the counter.'

'Don't worry, the apprentice sleeps at home. I know his grandfather. He's the one who used to . . .'

'Shhh.'

It was my turn to do the hissing. We were in front of the workshop. I could make out the gold lettering on the small display window and the plume of black ostrich feathers inside. The workshop had solid wooden double doors, tightly shut. The only way in that I could see was a slit of a window about eight feet above the ground. The frame looked old and wooden and probably the catch could be forced.

We stood looking up at it. I took a quick look up and down the street, jumped and managed to hook my fingers over the sill but couldn't get enough of a hold to pull myself up. I'd taken the precaution of wearing my climbing breeches. If we were caught, scandalising the population would be the least of our troubles.

'You could stand on my back, the way we do for rock chimneys.'

'No.'

Well over sixty, arthritis taking a hold and she seriously expected me to use her as a footstool. I looked around and saw an old bicycle leaning against a wall a few houses down.

'Can you steady it while I climb up?'

Standing on the saddle brought my eyes level with the

147

window frame. I'd half hoped that it would turn out to be impossible after all but it looked depressingly easy to force the catch. The lower part of the frame gaped by at least an inch and a thin metal bar on a peg was all that held it shut.

'Pass me the screwdriver, please.'

I pressed against the bottom of the metal bar. It lifted off the pin and clattered down. I paused, waiting to hear if the noise had disturbed anybody but the street was as quiet as . . . as the inside of a coffin. I passed the screwdriver back to Easyday, pushed up the window with one hand and took a firm grip on the sill with the other. By manoeuvring on the bike saddle I managed to get into a position where my head was holding the window open and I had a double grip on the sill. One more move and I was committed.

'Go on. What are you waiting for?'

She sounded like an urchin robbing an orchard. What could have possessed stiff, conventional Arthur, getting engaged to this? I launched myself from the security of the saddle and braced my good nailed climbing boots against the wall, thrusting head and shoulders through the window. From below Easyday hissed encouragement. I found myself peering down into the darkness of the undertaker's workshop.

One thing that should have occurred to me before then was that if you go through a narrow window head first you come down on the other side head first as well. I balanced uncomfortably for a while, head chest and arms inside, the rest outside until the prospect of getting caught in such a ridiculous position sent me slithering down the inside wall like a gecko that had lost faith in suction. Luckier than I deserved, I landed head first in a pile of wood shavings. Easyday, from outside, hooted like an owl. I hissed at her to be quiet and felt my way along the wall to the door. Only at that point I remembered there was a box of matches in my breeches pocket and it was by grace of the thieves' god they hadn't ignited while I was doing my gymnastics over the sill. I struck one of them and found that the heavy doors were locked and bolted, but the key was in the lock

148

and the bolts slid back after some tugging. I opened one of the doors a crack and Easyday slipped inside.

'Give me a light while I find the candles.'

After some fumbling we stood there each holding a candle, the light flickering round the walls, the carpenter's bench with its array of tools, the coffins. There were only three of them and luckily two were empty, their lids propped against the wall. Whatever they were doing with Gregory's body, it hadn't been released to the undertaker yet. Arthur's coffin was just as I'd last seen it, screwed down and sealed for the journey back to England which would never happen. The chemical smell I remembered was creeping round us, stronger than the scent of woodshavings or candles. I'd expected even Easyday to show a little emotion when she saw Arthur's coffin but all she said was:

'You'd better give that knife back to me. I'll show you.'

We fixed our candles on the stone floor in blobs of melted wax and she heated the knife blade.

'How many seals are there? Four. Start with this one.'

It was arthritis, not nerves, that defeated her. I took the knife from her, re-heated it and applied it to the thick seal of black wax.

'Not like that. It should slide through easily.'

I had to hack at it.

'The knife needs to be hotter.'

'You can't get it any hotter in candle flame. How did your governess manage?'

'She used a spirit lamp. You know, the kind they boil tea-kettles on.'

Tea-kettle and spirit lamp. If it wasn't the Gentian, it had to be in the tea. I'd drunk from the tea-pot, so something must have happened to it after that.

'If you're going to stand there daydreaming of course it's going to get cold. Let me have another try.'

In the end the job we did between us had nothing of the elegance of the schoolroom about it and she said her governess would have been ashamed of her. But we did get the seals sliced off, leaving me with the easier task of taking out the long brass screws.

'I don't think we'll have to lift the lid off. I remember it was tucked down the side. If we could just slide it sideways six inches or so, that should be enough.'

In spite of her determination, Easyday's hands couldn't manage heavy lifting and I wanted to spare her the sight of Arthur. She accepted what I said, probably more for the first reason than the second. I pushed the lid aside just far enough to show black crêpe lining and the edge of a shroud. Trying not to think about it too much I plunged my hand down the side of the coffin and my fingers came into contact almost at once with the smoothness of the waterproof wrapping.

'Right, got it. Now if we can push the lid back, I'll screw it down.'

It took longer than expected because of the difficulty of getting the screws lined up properly and I dropped one and had to scrabble for it on the floor. We did our best with the seals, but if anybody gave them more than a glance it would be obvious that they'd been tampered with. I had to hope that the consequences of this night's work wouldn't catch up with us before I'd settled other things. As there was no way of getting Easyday through the window we had to let ourselves out by the door and lock it from the outside. I climbed on to the bicycle saddle again to drop the key in through the window for the undertaker's benefit in the morning. He'd know there'd been intruders. Whether he'd notice that the journal was missing was another matter.

By the time we'd climbed back to the cabin the darkness was giving way to that thin-stretched, colourless sky that comes just before daylight. Even Easyday was tired and I made her sit down while I re-heated a saucepan of coffee and found a bone for the dog. All the time I was doing that the journal lay in its wrapping among the debris on her table. I didn't unwrap it until she'd finished her coffee.

'Do you want to see it?'

She took it from me and turned the pages, holding it close to the oil lamp. Several times something would catch her attention and she'd read, but it always seemed to be some detail about climbing. She gave little critical exclamations: 'Four hours for that little scramble – ridiculous' and 'Well, if the guides roped them up for that bit they can't have thought much of them.' I waited as patiently as I could. At last she closed the journal and sat with it on her knees, looking at me.

'Well, is it Arthur's writing or not?'

'I don't think it's Arthur's.'

My heart sank. After all, it wasn't enough.

'I don't suppose you've got anything in Arthur's handwriting we might compare it with?'

I wasn't hopeful. She wasn't the sort to keep old love letters, even if Arthur had been the sort to write them. She began shaking her head doubtfully, then:

'There was something. I asked him to get me a guide-book to the mountains. I think he wrote something in the front of it. It would be up there if I've still got it.'

She pointed to a tall cupboard against the wall. The top of it was in shadow, out of the range of the oil lamp, but I could make out piles of books.

'Have a look and see if you can find an old guide-book up there. It had a blue cover with a gold chamois on the front.'

There might have been a whole herd of them up there for all I could see in the dust and cobwebs. I'd had to stand on a chair to get at the books. When I pulled at the nearest one the whole pile of them came down on top of me in a cloud of dust and paper fragments and dead moths. Easyday stepped round the wreckage without comment and selected one book from it.

'That's the one.'

I picked myself up and looked over her shoulder as she opened it.

To my dear Daisy,
In the affectionate hope that her first holiday among the mountains will be a pleasant and instructive one. Arthur Mordiford, July 1880.

Just as well he couldn't have known how instructive.

'And this is definitely his writing?'

'Oh yes. He wrote it while I was there and then made a fuss because somebody had taken the blotter. You can see where it smudged.'

'It's not the same, is it?'

I picked up the journal. There were similarities between the two hands, as there would be with brothers who'd gone through the same education, but the writing in the journal was more flowing, with loops and curlicues, while the book inscription was narrow and compressed, as if written with the elbows tucked in. I'd been almost as sure when I saw the entry in Antoine's guide's book. Now, seeing the two together, I was certain of it. Easyday's eyes were sparkling but she tried not to be impressed.

'I told you all along, didn't I?'

'Yes, but this is the proof.'

To control my excitement I began to sort out the books scattered over the floor, intending to stack them back on the cupboard. They were a motley lot: a Victorian book on household management with the pages uncut, a well-thumbed French grammar, two tomes on the breeding and training of dogs. There were three volumes in the same elegant leather binding, thick and imposing with blocked and gold-tooled spines.

'Easyday, what are these?'

She picked her way among the fallen books and peered at them.

'Didn't know I'd got those. Oh, I remember now. Arthur brought a lot of books out with him, cases of them. He was supposed to be trying for a fellowship. Most of them went back to the family, but some got left.'

'These were Arthur's, you're quite sure of that?'

'Of course I am. Who else would want to read that nonsense except Arthur?'

I opened one of them, looked at the bookplate with college arms and Arthur's name, skimmed on through the evidence of close scholarly interest, the lines drawn in ink down the margins of certain passages, occasional notes in that cramped, elbows-in handwriting. It must have been a subject close to his heart or why else would he have brought on an alpine holiday with his brother and fiancée three volumes of Boswell's *Life of Samuel Johnson*?

'What's the trouble now?'

Easyday was standing over me as I crouched on the floor with the books.

'Let's sit down. I'm going to tell you a story. You knew them all. You can tell me whether you think I got it right or wrong.'

She gave me a glance and sat without a word, hands in her lap.

'There are two brothers. The elder one is upright and scholarly and not particularly warm-hearted. We presume that he's the one who's going to inherit the family business. The younger one's more passionate by nature, resents his brother perhaps. All the same, he accepts his invitation to join him on a climbing holiday. As luck would have it they find themselves staying at a house run by the most beautiful woman in Chamonix.'

I looked at Easyday. She was staring straight ahead, seeing something that wasn't in the room with us, giving quick little nods.

'Also as luck would have it, this woman is discontented. She married too young. Motherhood and the mountains are closing her in. She's pining for wide open streets and fashionable people strolling in the sunshine. Perhaps she sees some of that in Gregory.'

I'd used the name now. I could imagine him as a young man, prosperous and confident with a swagger about him that would be attractive to some women.

'Gregory's fancy free and a long way from home. Naturally he's attracted to Marie Martin. A beautiful Frenchwoman, older than he is, just what a young man on holiday would dream about. It's likely too that it's one way of scoring off his elder brother. Arthur will have the family money, but he doesn't sound like the kind of man who'd be attractive to women.'

Easyday shook her head slowly. She still wasn't looking at me.

'I can imagine Gregory playing a kind of game through those two weeks. On the one hand he'd want his brother to be aware of what was going on – that was part of the excitement for him. But he'd be in mortal terror that his parents might come to hear about it. I'm sure he'd be totally dependent on them for his spending money. The game was to make his brother jealous without giving him enough evidence to make trouble when they got home. A risky game, but then Gregory's nerve was good almost to the end.

'His downfall was that he couldn't help boasting, if only in his journal. It was a kind of personal code, apart from that one reference to the window in the valley, but quite enough to confirm Arthur's suspicions. My guess is that Arthur got his hands on Gregory's journal when they were camping on the first night out. To show his brother he knew what was going on he wrote a cruel quote out of Dr Johnson and put it back where he knew Gregory would find it. Guessing again, Gregory did find it, but not until the next night in the Grands Mulets hut. Some time that night, or possibly very early in the morning, the two brothers went out together and had an argument.

'I don't know why they climbed down to the snow. It might have been so that they could have their argument without waking up the others in the hut. It's even possible that Gregory had the idea of throwing the journal down a crevasse and Arthur followed him to snatch it back, as evidence to show their parents. Whatever happened, they were out there on the snow together and at least one of them had an ice-axe. Arthur got back possession of the journal. I can imagine him standing there, taunting Gregory with what would happen when they got home. Gregory probably hadn't intended to kill him, but he was scared and furious and the weapon was there. Once it was done he was too horrified even to get the journal back. He left it there in Arthur's pocket, dropped the ice-axe beside him and went back to the hut. If anybody noticed, they'd think he'd just been out on a call of nature.

154

'You could pity him for how he must have spent the rest of the night. He'd killed his brother. As soon as it was daylight the body would be discovered. Everything was over for him. Only it wasn't. He was saved by a piece of carelessness by a man who usually wasn't careless. Lucien Martin went out looking for Arthur before first light. He must have seen his body by the crevasse, tried to get to him too quickly and set off the avalanche. Only two people apart from him saw the blood on the snow, and they saw it in circumstances that made them leap to a reasonable but wrong conclusion. So they said nothing for thirty years.'

I thought of Pierre, having to grow up in the gossipy little town, keeping a secret all his life, not marrying. That stopped me feeling sorry for Gregory.

'The Mordiford family are quick thinkers. Gregory realised at once that the avalanche had saved him. He'd not only escaped being hanged for killing his brother, he'd unintentionally come out of the affair very well and was now the only son and heir. He prospered, married and probably lived an exemplary life, until the telegram arrived saying that Arthur had come down. No wonder he rushed out here and wanted to take the body home with him. That gash in Arthur's forehead was the only evidence against him.'

'Apart from the journal.'

It was lying there on the table beside her.

'Apart from the journal, and look how cleverly he dealt with that. He made it seem like an act of brotherly piety, just like this fuss about the body. Oddly enough though there was one thing he couldn't control and that was history repeating itself.'

'What?'

'His own son, doing very much what he'd done thirty years before, or trying to. Can you imagine how he must have felt when he saw Ben flirting with Sylvie Martin? It would have been bad enough in his eyes if they'd only been cousins, but they were half-brother and sister and he couldn't do anything about it without risking revealing the whole thing.'

155

Daylight was filtering into the room now, making the lamp look pale. The marmotte scrabbled in its box.

'Well, what happened then?'

'What do you mean, what happened then? We're at the end of the story.'

I was annoyed, thinking I deserved some applause. 'Do you think I'm right?'

'Oh yes.' She dismissed it almost in passing. 'I mean what happened to Gregory? Did he decide to kill himself after all? All came flooding back to him and he got remorseful?'

'No. The odd part is, I'd have said that was exactly what happened, apart from one thing. Somebody went to the trouble of setting a false trail by breaking that harmless bottle of Gentian. Ironic.'

'Why ironic?'

'Because if it hadn't been for that, I'd never have worked out who killed him.'

'You have?'

She sat forward suddenly in her chair.

'Almost, at any rate. The next thing is to find Pierre.'

EIGHTEEN

EASYDAY WOULDN'T HELP ME AT first. I had to do quite a lot of explaining and even then she was only reluctantly convinced.

'Can't you leave things as they are?'

'They don't stay as they are. They get worse.'

'Only because people keep interfering.'

'I never wanted to interfere. It all landed on top of me.'

'Anyway, I don't know any more than you do. Pierre's probably somewhere between the treeline and the snowline, anywhere on the mountain.'

Not a great help. Miles of steep mountainside, packed with screes, stonefalls and boulders.

'He'll keep away from the places where the tourists go. I shouldn't waste time looking for him near any of the chalets.'

I started sorting out my boots and pack.

'Why the hurry? Have a sleep first and go and look for him in the afternoon. It will be easier then.'

I thought she might be trying deliberately to delay me. Now that I knew so much I was impatient to put the rest of it in place.

'Why easier?'

'Everybody else comes down at the end of the afternoon, but he'll stay up there. If he shoots something he'll light a fire to cook it and you'll see the smoke from a long way off.'

I had to admit that it sounded sensible. She pointed to the dog, stretched out asleep on the floor.

'I'll lend you Bismarck if you like. About time he had a

decent walk. Pierre took his dog with him and Bismarck will find another dog if it's anywhere on the mountain.'

So I accepted both her advice and her dog. I slept for a few hours and woke around midday. Easyday was still in her cupboard, deeply asleep and snoring gently. I drank a coffee cold so as not to disturb her and found a piece of ancient climbing rope that would do as a dog's lead.

Bismarck seemed happy to come with me and we made our way down the mountain and through the town, avoiding the main streets and the big hotels because I didn't want to attract attention. A small grocer's shop provided cheese and pears for me and biscuits for Bismarck and I filled my water bottle at a pipe that channelled a spring into a stone trough on a street corner. A couple of black-dressed women gossiping beside it with their water-cans gave us curious glances but replied to my good afternoon civilly enough. They were talking about the widow Martin. Everybody in town probably was.

As we climbed up the other side of the valley we collected some more curious looks from holidaymakers on foot and mule-back, coming down in time for afternoon tea. It was far too hot for walking up mountains, with the sun blazing down on the path and a heavy feel in the air. I noticed cumulus clouds massing down the valley to the south-west. By the time we got to the path that runs more or less parallel to the valley towards the Mer de Glace the tourists had all gone down and we had it to ourselves. The sun was lower but the atmosphere was still hot and heavy. The stone spikes of the Chamonix Aiguilles that seemed airy and soaring from a distance made an oppressive wall when you climbed closer to them in weather like this. Even with no human beings around and birds stunned to silence by the heat it was still noisy, with falls of stones rattling down the couloirs. It was a reminder that although Bismarck and I were safe enough on the path we'd be at risk when we left it, and we'd have to leave it if we were going to find Pierre.

The temptation was to hurry and get out of the threatening feel of the place as soon as possible, but that wasn't what Pierre would do. The whole mountain would be as familiar to him as a desk-top to a clerk, not threatening at all. I made myself dawdle along, stopping every time a stream crossed the path to let Bismarck drink and pant a bit. He was the perfect dog for mountains, never lagging behind or going further ahead than I could see. Now and then he'd sit back on his haunches, body quivering and nose pointing, and I'd go tense. But I guessed he'd bark if he scented another dog and he didn't bark. To keep away from the crowds Pierre would probably have gone upslope from the path rather than down, so I watched every clump of rocks on my right carefully for any movement. They were casting long shadows as the sun went down and most of them could have hidden a dozen men. I thought I'd been a fool to imagine I could find him and when I looked back I saw the clouds were coming faster up the valley, with a bronze tinge to them that I didn't like.

I looked at my watch. Six o'clock. I'd give it another hour. At this time of year that should leave me just about enough time to get down to the valley before dark. We'd gone perhaps another mile when Bismarck sat down on the path in front of me, muzzle pointing up the slope, body quivering more than before. He made a high whining sound then a bark ripped out of him. He went on barking and the rock wall echoed the sound so that the whole valley seemed full of it. He stopped, still quivering, and another bark sounded from up the slope on our right. I thought at first it was an echo, but it was on a different note, higher than Bismarck's. Now that we had it my heart lurched and I knew I was breathing too quickly. I knelt down, hand on the dog's shoulders, listening. The barking had stopped after that first answering burst, almost certainly at somebody's command. I tried to judge the location of it, but that isn't easy in mountains.

'All right, boy, go and find him.'

I took a firm grip on the climbing rope attached to Bismarck's collar. There was no question of taking a direct line. Once we left the path we had to find the best way we

159

could round huge boulders, clumps of bilberries and patches of scree that slithered under Bismarck's scrabbling paws. He was puffing like bellows. I wished I'd thought to bring an ice-axe or even an alpenstock with me. It would have been reassuring if nothing else. When I climbed a flat rock to look round I saw that we were already several hundred feet above the path. There was no wisp or smell of smoke, just rocks, stubby bushes and sparse grass, and the roofs of the town a long way below. In the hotels guests would be changing into evening dress, waiters laying tables with crystal and silver. Then Bismarck gave one sharp bark and started whining again.

'What's up, boy? What's there?'

I spoke loudly, so that anybody in the vicinity would hear me. We hadn't come so far to avoid contact now, though the temptation was strong. It was hard to imagine that whatever came out of those rocks could be anything but a threat. As I stroked the dog I could feel his heart thumping even faster than mine. Then a voice, very close at hand, asked in English:

'Why are you here?'

Pierre was standing practically underneath my rock. He didn't look hostile exactly, but by no means pleased to see me either. His dog was beside him, growling at Bismarck until he told it to be quiet. It obeyed, but glared at Bismarck with teeth bared, probably much as Pierre would have liked to glare at me.

'I need to talk to you.'

'Is my mother still in prison?'

'Yes, but . . .'

'My sister?'

'Not in prison, if that's what you meant.'

Deliberately brutal of me, but I couldn't see that politeness would be much use at this point. He put out a hand to help me down from the rock but I ignored it and jumped. He led the way a few dozen yards across the slope to another clump of rocks, like the one I'd used for a look-out. One of them had lodged itself almost horizontally across two uprights, making a natural shelter underneath about the size of a railway carriage. Under it he'd stacked his pack, his crossbow and a blanket rolled up in a waterproof cape. There were the remains of a fire beside the rocks and a pile of small bones picked clean of meat.

I sat down on a handy rock and he took up a position facing me. He was unshaven, with strands of dry grass clinging to his hair and a smear of wood ash down the side of his nose, shirt open at the neck. His eyes looked brighter than down in the valley but it was a dangerous brightness, like an animal wondering whether to run away or go for the throat.

'I've been to see Antoine Bregoli,' I said.

Our dogs shuffled into opposing positions alongside the rocks, eyes locked on each other. Occasionally one of them would let out a low growl, echoing the thunder that was rumbling down the valley.

'You can guess what I found out from him, but it's not the whole story of what happened to your father. You've never known the whole story.'

I wished he'd say something. He didn't.

'May I tell it to you now?'

He still said nothing, didn't move, so I told it to him, very much as I'd told it to Easyday. There was no point in trying to spare him on the subject of Gregory Mordiford and his mother. As I talked I was aware that the thunder was getting louder and the great bronze-tinged clouds had moved up until they were sitting on the mountain peaks, making a lid for the valley.

'You told me yourself that people were coming and going all night. Nobody would have thought anything of it if Arthur and Gregory went out one after the other. Of course your father would have woken up before first light because he was responsible for the whole party. He'd notice before anybody else did that Arthur was missing. He went out and as soon as there was enough light he'd see the body on the snow, by the crevasse. He wouldn't know if Arthur was alive or dead. His guide's instinct, his good guide's instinct, was to get down to his monsieur as soon as possible. Because of this he made a mistake. He tried to take a line across what turned out to be an unstable slope and – you know the rest.'

'I know the rest.'

His voice was as grim as the dog's growl. I thought he couldn't have understood me, that I'd been going too fast for him.

'Monsieur Martin, do you understand what I've been telling you? You've believed all these years that your father murdered his monsieur. He didn't. It was his own brother who killed him.'

'I know.'

I nearly fell off my rock. Of all the things he might have said, this was the least expected.

'How did you know?'

I felt cheated too. I'd gone to such trouble to bring him what I thought would be good news.

'Monsieur Gregory told me.'

'Gregory? Gregory told you himself? When? Why?'

Big drops of rain were beginning to fall, spreading themselves in blots over the warm rock. I noticed them, but they might have been in another world. In the one I'd just entered, raindrops might as well fall upwards.

'Up by the Glacier des Bossons, when I was showing him where we found the body.'

'You're saying that after all these years Gregory just broke down and admitted it to you?'

He hesitated, made up his mind.

'I'll tell you, but we'd better get under shelter.'

The raindrops were coming faster, the rocks dark and wet all over. We ran and wedged ourselves under the tilted slab, each with our backs against one of the upright rocks for all the world like two passengers in a railway carriage. The dogs decided that this was enough encouragement for a guarded truce, stopped glaring at each other and came in with us.

'I've told you my story, so now please tell me yours, from the time that you and the Mordiford men went on up the path together.'

He thought about it, taking his time, and began haltingly.

'You know there were four of us, Monsieur Gregory, his son, his nephew and me. We went up the path together, quite slowly. You know it wasn't far. We came to the place and I showed him exactly where his brother's body had been found. I pointed out the way it had come down the glacier.'

That tallied with what I'd been told.

'He hadn't admitted killing Arthur then?'

'No.'

'How did he behave?'

'Very troubled, nervous. You could see something was wrong.'

'Were his son and nephew with you when you were talking to him?'

'Near, but not with us.'

'When did he tell you?'

'Not then, not quite. I walked up the path a little way on my own. I thought it was right to leave them together. It was a family matter after all.'

'And at that point you still believed that your father had killed Arthur Mordiford?'

He looked at me and bent to give his dog the kind of stroke meant to be calming, but at that time the dog was quiet enough.

'Yes.'

He said it to the ground. In all his life, that might have been the first time he admitted it.

'Go on.'

'I went just round the bend out of sight, but still near enough to hear if they called me.'

'Did they call?'

'No. So I waited for a while and then I went back down to them.'

'How long?'

'Perhaps ten minutes.'

Lightning jagged the mountainside not far below us. Thunder rolled round our shelter.

163

'Monsieur Gregory came up to me. He looked terrible, like a dead man. His face was pale and he was sweating. Before I could ask him what was wrong, he said it.'

'Tell me exactly.'

'He was speaking in English. It was hard for me to understand him at first because his voice was shaking, so he said it twice. He said this, exactly: "Monsieur, you have a right to know that I killed my brother Arthur." Then again: "I killed my brother." '

'Did you believe him?'

There was a long pause, not from doubt but because he was searching for the right words.

'From the way he said it, it was impossible not to believe it. He didn't want to say it, but he made himself say it all the same. If you'd heard him, you'd have believed it too.'

'Were you angry?'

'I'm angry now when I think of it. I wasn't angry then.'

He gestured at the cloud clamped above the valley like a lid of perforated zinc, cutting out the light and pouring down water that hissed into the ground outside our shelter.

'It was like that. All my life I'd been living with the idea that my father killed him. When it went, it was like the cloud going.'

'Gregory Mordiford could have lifted that cloud at any time in the last thirty years.'

'I know. That's why I'm angry with him when I think about it now. I wasn't then.'

'Did you say anything to Ben or Hector at the time?'

'No.'

'Did they say anything to you?'

'No.'

'Do you think he'd told them what he told you?'

'Yes. I know he must have told his son at least. On the way down I heard him say to Monsieur Benedict that he wasn't to tell his sister until afterwards.'

'Until after what?'

'I don't know.'

Dusk had come early. I couldn't see his face any more,

except in silhouette. The rain was slanting in under the horizontal rock and making our dry space narrower, so that the dogs had to press themselves against our feet to keep away from the wet. There was a smell of soaked earth, of dog, of sweat.

'Do you think he poisoned himself?'

'I don't know.'

I could tell from his voice that he didn't.

'Did you know there wasn't any poison in the Gentian bottle?'

He hadn't known. He moved suddenly in the confined space, his knee making contact with mine.

'Two of the mule-boys drank from it as well. So your mother and Sylvie are only as suspect as the rest of us – no less, no more.'

I let that sink in for a while.

'Were you sure they were guilty? Was that why you ran off?'

'I was ashamed. I'd lost my monsieur, just like my father did and with the same family. That had never happened to anybody before. How could I walk round the town knowing what people were saying about me?'

'But for heaven's sake, you'd just found out that your father didn't kill his monsieur.'

'People didn't know that.'

'Why didn't you tell them?'

I couldn't see him looking at me, but I could feel it.

'Would you have told them in my place? Would you?'

'Why not?'

'Tell them that my mother had been the mistress once of the man who'd just died? Tell them that, when she was already suspected of killing him? Would that be a good idea, do you think?'

'Probably not.'

'Well then, what could I do?'

The thunder and lightning were moving away up the valley, but the rain was still pouring down. We sat in silence for a long time until his breathing became slower and calmer and he let his head drop forward into his hands.

'You'll have to go down to the valley some time, you know.'

Not there and then, of course. We'd already accepted without needing to discuss it that he, I and the dogs would have to spend the night where we were. Even if the rain stopped it would be madness to go down a steep wet path in the dark.

'Yes, some time.'

Later he apologised because he had no food to offer me.

'We ate the partridge, the dog and I.'

We all four of us shared the food in my pack then settled down to sleep on our narrow slice of dry mountainside, I wrapped in his blanket with my back against one of the rocks, he hunched in his waterproof cape against the opposite rock and the dogs piled in between us. It was, in its way, as decorous as a chapel Sunday though that might not be the way they'd react to it down in the hotels.

I said to him before we slept:

'You should come down tomorrow. I think it's going to be all right.'

He didn't answer.

NINETEEN

IN THE END BISMARCK AND I went down on our own in the morning, but I'd wrested a promise from Pierre that he'd follow at some time over the next twenty-four hours. The discussion, over the last pear and mouthfuls of stream water that had passed for breakfast, had at least brought out the other reason for Pierre's flight into the mountains. He'd managed to keep the story of Gregory's confession to himself during his first session with the examining magistrate but was scared that he'd trip up and reveal it if he was questioned again. Like most open-air men, he had a suspicion of officials behind desks that amounted to panic. Not surprisingly when you considered that he'd spent most of his life concealing something. When I asked him why it was so important that the story shouldn't be known he wouldn't answer directly but his evasions made it clear: he thought it would make things look even more black for his mother. His reasoning seemed to be that if she'd come under suspicion of murder for having a love affair with Gregory's brother the situation would have been worse when the magistrate knew the more complicated story.

There was a question I should have asked him, but didn't. Do you think your mother poisoned Gregory Mordiford? I was sure he did believe that, and at present I didn't have the evidence to convince him or anybody else otherwise. There was one fact that stuck out from his story. He hadn't said anything about Gregory's confession, and neither had Ben or Hector. On Pierre's evidence, Ben knew about the confession and it was almost unthinkable

167

that Hector didn't know too. So why had neither of them said anything? It could be that they'd decided to protect Gregory's reputation posthumously, but I needed to be sure.

I paused before I got down to inhabited country to tidy up as best I could, washed all over at a waterfall made rumbustious by the night's storm and swapped my breeches for a skirt. It was creased and dusty from being used as a pillow, so didn't improve matters much. Bismarck watched from a rock as I tried to put up my damp hair with the few hairpins that had managed to cling to it through yesterday's wanderings. We were a disreputable couple as we continued our journey and I was glad it was too early to meet polite tourist traffic. The parties of climbers we passed on their way up were a different matter and wouldn't think it eccentric to bivouac on the hill in a storm. Some of the guides with them recognised Easyday's dog and called out good morning to him and to me. When we got to town I managed to dig out a few francs from the bottom of my pack, sticky with pear juice, and treated Bismarck and myself to milky coffee and croissants in a back-street café.

At the earliest reasonable hour to call I presented myself at the reception desk of the Hôtel du Mont Blanc, leaving the dog in the care of a hotel gardener. Hector Tenby was already at the desk, talking urgently to a clerk who kept shaking his head regretfully. When he turned and saw me he said without preamble:

'Miss Bray, we're worried to distraction. Have you seen Ben?'

His hair was almost as disordered as mine and there were dark circles round his eyes.

'No. I thought he was going to Paris to meet Beatrice's cousin.'

'So did we. But Bertha – that's the cousin – arrived yesterday on the evening train and no Ben. She says he telegraphed her before she left London saying she was to come on alone and he'd explain later. But he specifically told us he was going to meet her. That was the whole point of going to Paris.'

I could understand his worry and knew he had cause for it. I registered too that Beatrice, torn between loyalty to her brother and her fiancé, had not yet come down decisively against Ben.

'I'll go up and see Beatrice if she'd like me to, but could we have a talk first?'

He led the way into the garden. It smelt fresh after the rain and the mountains were as clear as crystal. I wished my head felt the same.

'There's something that might have a bearing on Ben's behaviour.'

'Then I wish you'd tell me what it is. Goodness knows, I've got used to Ben's impulsiveness over the years, but this beats all.'

'I think you know what it is already.'

He stopped walking and stared at me. I watched his expression change.

'Ben must have been quite shaken by what happened up at the Glacier des Bossons.'

'So was his sister, so was I, so were you for that matter. None of the rest of us thought it justified our disappearing completely.'

'I wasn't thinking of Gregory's death.'

'Oh.' He started walking again, more slowly. 'May I ask what you were thinking of?'

'Gregory said something to Ben when the four of you were up there on your own. To Pierre as well. You were very close to your uncle. I'd be amazed if he hadn't said it to you too.'

'Oh.'

The exclamation wasn't shock, more an acknowledgement that circumstances had changed.

'It must have been Pierre Martin who told you.'

'That doesn't matter. I'd got there anyway. I knew it was almost certain that Gregory had murdered his brother. What I didn't know was that he'd actually admitted it.'

'How did you know?'

Seeing no reason not to answer, I told him about the entry in Antoine's guide-book and the volumes of Boswell in Easyday's cabin.

'I knew you were being over-modest, Miss Bray. You told me you had no ambitions to be a detective.'

'That was the truth, but there's a woman suspected of murder.'

'You think it will help Madame Martin if the authorities know she and Gregory were lovers and he deserted her?'

'I don't know if it will help her or not, but surely the more facts that come out, the better.'

'That's hardly been the Mordiford family motto so far.'

'Far from it. And there's somebody else involved besides Marie Martin.'

'Pierre?'

I was surprised by his promptness. Surely gossip about my night on the mountain wasn't going round the town already.

'The fact is, he's been living under a cloud all his professional life because he thought his father killed Arthur. At least one of the old guides thought so too and I'm sure a rumour got round. Even if you think it won't help Madame Martin to talk about Gregory's confession, don't you think the family owes it to her son?'

He sighed.

'Yes. I'd thought of that.'

That was implicitly a confirmation of what I already knew from Pierre. Gregory had confessed, and Hector as well as Ben knew it.

'I've come to much the same conclusion about it as you have – that it's only fair to let it be known. But it must, it simply must, wait until the funeral's over and I can get Beatrice out of this confounded town. What I'd intended to do was have Gregory and Arthur buried as soon as we could, then get her out with as little fuss as possible. Once I knew Beatrice was safely on her way with her cousin I intended to speak to the examining magistrate and do what I could to put things right as regards Pierre. I must admit I'd planned a role for you there.'

'What?'

'You know the town better than we do. You could have

170

put the word round where it mattered most, among the guides.'

'I could do that, yes.'

'But Ben's the problem. We can't bury his father until he chooses to turn up and God knows where he's gone. It really is totally infuriating of the man. To be honest, he's always had trouble facing up to responsibility.'

I refrained from saying it seemed to be a family trait. We reached a trellis of pink roses, stared at it for a while, turned.

'You were surprised by Gregory's confession?'

He took a few scrunching steps along the gravel path before replying.

'To anybody else I should say yes. That's the line I'll take when I see the examining magistrate. But I don't think you'd believe me, would you?'

A few more steps.

'I was surprised. I didn't expect it to be as bad as that, but perhaps I wasn't quite as surprised as I should have been. I knew something was badly wrong from his reaction when those two telegrams arrived in the office, so I suppose I was looking out for this. Then when he insisted on signing that paper about Sylvie being Arthur's daughter, I couldn't understand why he was doing it. I sensed at the time he didn't believe it, but I couldn't see what hold the old lady had over him.'

'An even bigger one than she realised. She couldn't have known about the murder.'

'He thought she knew, though. Looking back, I'm sure of that.'

He stopped again, picked a shoot off a veronica plant and shredded it leaf by leaf without realising what he was doing.

'If you'd seen the way he looked when he told us, Ben and me, like somebody dead already but just brought back to life long enough to say what he had to say.'

He shivered and let leaves drop on the path.

'Why do you think he decided to confess then?'

'God knows. I suppose something snapped at last.'

'Do you think Beatrice guesses?'

'I'm quite sure she doesn't and I'm going to make certain she never knows, if I have to lie from now to the end of my life. Can you imagine what it would do to a sensitive woman like Beatrice, knowing that about her father?'

I offered to go up and see her if he thought she wanted it.

'I'd be very grateful if you would. But please don't say anything to her. She respected her father. I honestly think that if she knew what he'd done it would drive her almost insane.'

We went up in the lift together but when he knocked gently on the door a plump and anxious-looking woman put her head round it, finger to her lips. Cousin Bertha. She came out to the corridor, closing the door behind her, to whisper to us.

'I've got her to go sleep at last, poor love. I've drawn the curtains and I'm just going to go and stop those maids clattering about downstairs.'

She and Hector went down to deal with them and I went, with some relief, to collect Bismarck from the gardener and make my report to Easyday.

At six o'clock I was back outside Beatrice's door. Cousin Bertha let me in, shaking her head when I asked if there was any more news of Ben. The curtains were still half-drawn, cutting out most of the afternoon sun. Beatrice was sitting in an armchair wearing slippers and a blue silk dressing-gown, the smell of Eau de Cologne hanging round her. The look she gave me was half pleading, half scared.

'Have you . . . ?'

I shook my head.

'Bertha, could you go down and see about tea for Miss Bray. They take such ages to answer the bell.'

As soon as the door closed behind her obedient cousin Beatrice came running to me and flung herself crying into my arms.

'Oh what shall I do? What shall I do?'

'Have you heard from Ben again?'

172

'No. I was hoping that Bertha would know something, but she doesn't. Oh, what do you think he's doing? Is he in trouble?'

Whatever trouble he was in, he was only making it worse, but there was no point in saying that to Beatrice. I let her have her cry then got her to sit down in the armchair.

'You haven't told Hector?'

'No, how could I? He's angry enough with Ben as it is because he thinks he's gone away and not said anything. I hate keeping things from him, but Ben said I mustn't tell him and he must have a reason, mustn't he? Oh Miss Bray, do you think Ben's done something . . . something well, silly . . . ?'

Her voice trailed away but her eyes said it all. Would murder count as 'something silly' in her vocabulary?

'What kind of thing?'

'He was angry with Papa over not letting him go to art school in Paris, then that awful woman. I'm sure he's sorry now . . . for being angry, but if only he'd come back. Do you think I should go to meet him? I was lying awake all night, thinking of him meeting all the trains and me not being on them. Perhaps I should do what he wants and go to him. I might be able to persuade him to come back with me.'

I told her that I thought this wouldn't be a very good idea.

'But what can I do? You don't know what it's like, sitting here wondering, not being able to do anything.'

'I don't suppose you have an address for him in Paris?'

She shook her head.

'You're probably right, then – he'll be meeting all the trains. Do you want me to go?'

It had come to me on an impulse, but when I thought about it, it seemed the best way of cutting this knot.

'Oh would you, would you? I'd be so grateful I'd . . . I don't know what to say.'

'I'm afraid I'll need some money for the fare. Have you got any?'

'Oh yes, yes.'

She ran to a drawer, pressed a wad of notes into my hands.

'Is that enough? You'll never know how grateful I am to you. Could you go this evening?'

'I think I've already missed the night train. I'll go first thing tomorrow, if you like.'

'Yes. I'm sure he'll be there waiting, whenever it is. Tell him I'm all right, but so worried about him. Do bring him back with you if you can.'

I made no promises on that score and escaped from the hotel without meeting Hector again. I discovered that the morning train left at breakfast time so spent the night at the pension by the station, using Beatrice's money. I hadn't liked taking it from her in the circumstances, but what could I do?

TWENTY

THE JOURNEY TOOK MOST OF the daylight hours and I arrived at the Gare de Lyon at eleven o'clock at night. As soon as I set foot on the platform the smoke and the stale, pent-up air of the city hit me like a stupefying gas. At this time of night our arrival was no great event. A few tired porters sauntered, looked disdainfully at my small pack and travel-worn appearance and didn't bother to ask. I walked slowly down the platform towards the barrier and saw him long before he saw me. That white suit stood out like a seagull on ploughland. He was scanning the few dozen passengers leaving the train and even when he looked in my direction his eyes slid on without recognising me. Naturally it was his sister he expected, if anybody. I was no more than twenty yards away by the time it hit him. He was standing close to a gas lamp so I could see the expression on his face, a flash of alarm at first, then a deliberate setting into the amused cynicism that seemed to be his reaction to most things. He raised his hat with an exaggerated gesture.

'On your way home?'

'Looking for you.'

He smiled. 'Come to drag me back, have you? I suppose that was Hector's idea.'

'No, your sister's.'

'Did she show Hector the telegram?'

It wasn't my business to reassure him.

'Beatrice is extremely worried about you. She wants you to come back.'

'Why won't she come to me here? You and Hector

175

persuaded her not to, I suppose. A mistake.'

'Is there somewhere we can go and talk?'

The ticket collector was fidgeting, wanting us out of the way so that he could close the barrier. Ben hesitated, probably trying to work out whether to agree or walk away.

'I have a room in a hotel over there, if you can call it a hotel, but I can hardly invite a lady there at this time of night.'

He looked me up and down, taking in every crease and lost hairpin.

'Not even a lady of your advanced views.'

His manners hadn't improved since he'd arrived in Paris but I was already noticing a difference in him, a swagger that hadn't been there in Chamonix. He'd been there under protest as his father's son. Now, for better or worse, he was out in the world on his own. It was a wide world too. He'd soon have his father's money and could go anywhere. But there was a desperation about his swagger. His eyes were too bright and he was talking too loudly. He didn't seem drunk but I caught a whiff of absinthe on his breath.

'There's a café near here where the railway people go. I've become quite an habitué, waiting for all these trains.'

He led the way out of the station and down a side street with tall terraces of houses on either side and a smell of rubbish gently decomposing in the warm night air. It was dark except for a spillage of light on to the pavement half way down. As we came nearer the smell of coffee fought with the rubbish but managed no better than a draw. The café was a stark room with bare wooden tables and chairs, lit by unshaded electric light bulbs. A large unshaven man, shirt open at the neck and waistcoat unbuttoned, presided behind a zinc counter. There were half a dozen or so customers, a few men in railway uniforms, a small dark man with a pitted face, slumped with his cheek on the table, two women talking to each other at a table by the door, showing their ankles in pink silk stockings, but more from habit than hope. Their plumed hats were placed carefully on chairs beside them, the feathers bent and dusty.

We sat at a table by the wall.

'Wine?'

'Coffee please, large and black.'

He bought an absinthe for himself, poured water in and watched, apparently absorbed, as the milky clouds spread.

'I tried to paint that effect once. It's almost impossible.'

He jerked his eyes away from it and looked up at me.

'Well?'

'Before you left Chamonix you paid a visit to Sylvie Martin. You asked her one question.'

That surprised him but he recovered quickly. 'You have been thorough in your investigations about me, haven't you? Or perhaps you were hiding under the tablecloth.'

'She wouldn't tell me what the question was. I thought I'd guessed. I know now I was wrong.'

'How unusually humble of you.'

'I thought you'd asked Sylvie if she'd marry you.'

He gave an odd, twisted smile to the clouds in the absinthe.

'And what made you decide you were wrong?'

'Something I found out later. After all, you could hardly marry your half-sister.'

Another smile, not at me. 'The ancient Egyptians did.'

'You wanted something urgently from Sylvie, urgent enough to risk missing your train. You wanted to know if your father and your uncle might have quarrelled over her mother as young men.'

I waited for him to react.

'Go on.'

'I think Sylvie probably told you the truth, just as her mother told her – that Gregory had an affair with Marie Martin but Arthur didn't.'

I watched his face as he made a decision. It certainly wasn't a decision to trust me, simply to throw out a piece of information as an angler throws out bait.

'As it happens, you're quite right. Mademoiselle Sylvie Martin is an admirably direct woman. Don't you find the

177

French are so much less hypocritical about these things?'

He leaned back and took a sip of absinthe, very much the man of the world, but when he tried to cross one white-trousered leg casually over the other it twitched and jumped. He smoothed it with his hand.

'So then you had the whole story. You knew that your father murdered his brother and you knew what the quarrel had been about.'

He looked into his drink and murmured, 'Hector's told you quite a lot, hasn't he?'

I didn't correct him.

'Did your father's confession come as a shock to you?'

'A surprise.'

'How did he tell you?'

'I was standing on the path, smoking a cigarillo and wishing that the whole tedious business were over. He came up to me and to be honest I thought he was going to be sick. Then he just came out with it, no warning: "Everything must be in your hands from now on. I killed my brother and when we get down to the town I'm going to admit it to the authorities." '

'He said that, about admitting it?'

'Have I discovered another gap in your knowledge? Yes, that's what he said.'

'What did you say?'

'What could I say? To be honest, I'm not sure I took it in at first. I suppose I thought the strain from all that morbid stuff had got to him. I probably said "there, there", or noises to that effect.'

'When did you decide he was telling the truth?'

'When he killed himself.'

'You think it was suicide?'

'Don't you?'

'Did you tell the examining magistrate that?'

'He didn't ask my opinion. He only wanted to know what I heard and saw.'

'But neither you nor Hector told him about your father's confession.'

'I can't speak for Hector. I didn't.'

178

'Why not?'

'I suppose I wanted time to think round things.'

'Even though Madame Martin was in prison?'

'I don't think they'd arrested her then. Anyway, it's hardly as if they're going to chop her head off in the morning, is it? The trial will probably take weeks.'

He drained his glass and pushed his hair out of his eyes. Two of the railwaymen put on their caps, said good-night to the man at the counter and walked out, giving long stares to the women by the door as they went.

'You remember your father asked for you at the end?'

He nodded, carefully looking into my eyes. His pupils were large and black.

'He was trying very hard to say something to you. Do you know what it was?'

He shook his head.

'Probably nothing important. Never was.'

His stare almost pleaded with me to be shocked.

'He thought it was important.'

'He thought a lot of things were important.'

'Once he was dead you decided to believe him about killing his brother. You thought you'd guessed the motive so you talked to Sylvie to confirm it. Is that right?'

'More or less.'

'Were you shocked when you knew?'

He glanced round the dismal café, the man still slumped on the table, the two women talking with their heads close together.

'This isn't the place or the time of day for hypocrisy. I was pleased.'

'Why pleased?'

'Why not? The gods saw fit to have me born into one of the dullest of all the tribal groups on the face of the earth – the English mercantile middle class. My father and my grandfather spent blameless lives exporting clocks and kitchen gear to the colonies and getting sheepskins back, going to church on Sundays, making marriages without a spark of passion in them and building up their bank balances. From the time I toddled it was made clear to me that I was expected to grow up and do likewise. What sort of background is that for an artist?'

'A financially secure one, at any rate.'

'Then all of a sudden I have a father – or rather a late father – who seems to have broken most of the Ten Commandments and committed the sin of Cain in just about the most spectacular way possible. It's like finding fresh air and a view where you thought there was only wallpaper.'

He was still talking to shock, but there was a passion about him I hadn't seen before.

'I'll admit something else to you. When I knew this about my father I felt closer to him than I'd ever felt in my life. I wanted to have him alive again so that we could talk about it. I'd have liked to know what he felt like when he'd done it and how he could go back to that interminable drawing-room and counting-house life as if nothing had happened. We might have understood each other in a way we never did while he was alive.'

The two women near the door came to a decision, stood up wearily and began to pin on their hats. The slumped man raised his head a few inches from the table and asked them, with obscenities, if trade had been good tonight. They ignored him and went out.

'I don't suppose Beatrice would feel the same.'

He scowled.

'We're not talking about Beatrice.'

'She asked me to come here. She wants me to persuade you to go back and talk to her.'

'Oh yes.'

He was sceptical. I could hardly blame him.

'Will you come back?'

He shook his head.

'Get her to come to me here. Come back with her if she won't travel alone. If you really want to help her it would be the best thing you could do for her.'

'Why?'

'That's none of your business. Just bring her.'

'Why won't you come back?'

'I've got business here.'

'What kind of business?'

'Family business. Isn't that what everybody's been nagging me to do all my life?'

He signed to the man at the counter to bring more coffee and another absinthe. While they were being brought to us he stared at me, deliberately offensive. I stared back.

'You're on the wrong side, Miss Bray, you know that?'

'I wasn't aware of being on anybody's side.'

He laughed and said nothing.

'Unless you mean that I don't believe your father killed himself. I don't think you believe it either.'

He was trying to pour a trickle of water from the jug into his absinthe and almost managed it with a steady hand, but not quite.

'You say your father told you that he intended to go down and confess. Wouldn't it have been awkward for several people if he'd done that? You for one.'

'I've told you how I felt about it.'

'One version. In that version you have the advantage of inheriting all your father's money with the secret satisfaction of being the son of a murderer. Would the satisfaction be as great if you didn't inherit?'

'I'm his only son.'

'Yes, but he only inherited the family money because Arthur was murdered. A man can't profit by his crime in law. Does the same apply to a man's son?'

I didn't know, but judging by the expression on his face, neither did he. There was anxiety in his eyes.

'It's a much clearer situation now that your father's dead without confessing.'

'Are you saying I killed him?'

'I'm simply asking myself who had the greatest reason not to want a public confession from your father. You might be one. Madame Martin's another. Then there's Sylvie.'

He showed no concern when I mentioned Madame Martin, but Sylvie was another matter.

'What would it matter to her?'

'Your father had promised them money. If he were dead

they might think they stood some chance of getting it from his executors, with that signed statement. If he were alive and found guilty of murder it was much less likely.'

'Ingenious.'

His face was back in control. I probed what seemed to be the tender point.

'Some people would say Sylvie and her mother were playing a cruel game, using you to work on your father.'

'They knew what they wanted.'

'Cynical, wouldn't you say, making Arthur Sylvie's father when at least two of them must have known it was Gregory.'

'Sylvie didn't know it was Gregory. Her mother didn't tell her until after the paper was signed.'

It was his first unguarded remark. The strain or the drink must be working on him.

'She thought it was Arthur too. For goodness' sake, you don't think she'd have been making up to me like that if she knew we were half-brother and sister? Or me to her?'

'So it must have come as a shock to her, the night before the picnic.'

'So Sylvie's the suspect now, is she? So shocked to find that Gregory's her father after all that she slips poison in the Gentian and hands the glass to him?'

He was trying to keep up his cynical, bantering tone but finding it difficult. To keep him off balance I said:

'The poison wasn't in the Gentian. It must have been in the tea.'

I'd wanted to shock him and it worked. He'd had the water jug in his hands when I said it but now he thumped it back on the table. He stared while I told him about Nico and the mule-boy.

'He's been bribed.'

'If somebody were trying bribery they'd have chosen a more intelligent witness.'

'Beatrice brewed that tea. She was always fussing with that damned teapot.'

'Yes.'

He stared at me for a long time and I could feel the

defences being rebuilt. He took a long drink and shrugged.

'Well, thank you for that.'

'Thank you?'

'Yes, I can see what the game is now. Shall we go?'

He got to his feet, pushing his chair back with a scraping sound and flung some change on to the table. His sleeve caught his half-full glass and it fell and shattered on the floor.

'Like the bottle of Gentian,' I said. 'Somebody went to a lot of trouble to make sure it got broken.'

The two remaining customers were looking at us. The large patron moved out from behind the counter rolling up his sleeves, weary but businesslike.

'Out monsieur, out. You too, madame.'

We moved out of the light into the dark street and turned back towards the station. A rat came out of a pile of rubbish like a pip from a squeezed orange but apart from that there wasn't another creature in sight.

'A rough area.'

Ben's tone was conversational again, but with a tremor in it. He pushed his panama firmly down on his head.

'You know, the first night here a couple of ruffians tried to steal my wallet. So as soon as the shops opened I got this.'

His hand went into his pocket and came out holding a knife like a small dagger with a broad blade. His other hand suddenly shoved me in the chest, pushing me, half-falling, into a shop doorway. Before I could get my balance his weight was on me, holding me pinned against the door. I felt the knife against my neck, smelt the absinthe on his breath and, absurdly, the odour of a boiled beetroot we must be crushing underfoot.

'People get killed in streets like this and nobody worries.'

I threw my weight on to the door, but it was solid. He got his left hand round the back of my neck and pulled so that the knife-point sank in another millimetre.

'There's a train back to England in the morning. You should be on it, don't you think? There's really nothing more for you to do here.'

I very much dislike being threatened, especially by

people who are as bad at it as Ben Mordiford. I made a little whimpering sound as if in mortal fear and let myself slide down the door. His grasp on the back of my neck slackened and the knife-tip only grazed my skin as I went down. About halfway to the ground I suddenly straightened up and drove my knee into him. As he staggered back with a gasp, hat and knife flying, I remembered Easyday's advice on the proper conduct of ladies and stamped hard on his instep for good measure. History certainly seemed to have a way of repeating itself for the Mordifords. When I looked back from the top of the street he was still kneeling in the middle of the pavement among the rubbish. I spent the remaining few hours of the night upright on a station bench, waiting for the morning train back.

By the morning he'd recovered enough to watch me walking down the platform, cramped and stiff, and getting into a second class compartment of the train to Chamonix. From the corner of my eye I caught a glimpse of a white suit by a tobacco kiosk near the barrier. I found a seat facing back up the platform and watched without surprise, when five minutes before the train's departure, he joined it as well. First class, near the end. He must have realised by now that if he intended to prevent my return he'd need more effective methods. To give him no chance of practising them I got into conversation with the people in my compartment and made sure I wasn't without company in all the long, hot day's journey back to the mountains. I was aware of him watching me when we changed trains and kept the length of the platform between us.

When we arrived back at Chamonix, after dark, I let him go first and watched from outside the station, making no secret of it, as he got into a cab. It drove off at a trot, although not in the direction of the Hôtel du Mont Blanc, and after watching it out of sight I walked with my pack up the path through the pinewoods to Easyday's.

TWENTY-ONE

SHE WAS STILL AWAKE, SITTING over the fire with Bismarck, and wanted to know where I'd been gallivanting off to, as she put it. I told her in detail and her eyes gleamed when she heard about the knife.

'Ben thought he was in control of the situation until I told him the poison wasn't in the Gentian. He didn't get really angry until I told him it must have been in the tea.'

'But you told me you drank a cup of tea from that pot yourself.'

'I certainly drank a cup of tea, and I think I see now how that was done. But I'm as near certain as can be that the brew in that tea-pot included the *tue-loup* from Beatrice's collection.'

'What happened to the rest of the tea?'

'It was poured away. You don't carry half a pot of cold tea down a mountain with you.'

When I thought about it I could picture Beatrice distractedly swirling the tea round and round, eyes on her father, then pouring it away on the grass.

'I suppose I might be able to lead the police to the remains of it, but there's been a rain storm since then, probably more than enough to wash tea dregs away.'

'Then you can't prove it.'

'Except that nothing else makes sense.'

Later, when the fire had burned low and Bismarck was snoring, I asked Easyday about the procedure for booking a guide.

'It's strictly by rota. You have to hire the guide at the top of the list.'

'No good to me.'

'There is a way round it. If you're a woman climbing alone then you're allowed to hire the guide you want, whether he's at the top of their list or not. A sort of *Droit de Madame*, you might say.'

She chuckled. 'You're going to make yourself very conspicuous, marching in there and demanding him.'

'Conspicuous is exactly what I want to be.'

When the guides' bureau opened in the morning, I was there at the head of the queue. The place was as crowded as I could have wished with climbers talking to each other in three languages, loud and confident English predominating as usual. I spoke English for once myself, loudly enough for my voice to carry over the rest.

'I want to hire a guide to go up to the Grands Mulets hut tomorrow. I intend to spend the night there and paint the sunrise.'

A few sniggers, nothing more. English painting ladies clustered on every accessible ridge in Chamonix at sunrise and sunset, commonplace as starlings on city ledges.

'Certainly, madame.' The guide reached for his list.

'There's one guide in particular I want.'

A few more sniggers, but again there was nothing particularly unusual about that.

'His name, madame?'

'Monsieur Pierre Martin.'

Instant silence. I could feel every pair of eyes in the place turning towards me. The consistent record of Martins, father and son, in losing their English clients must have been the talk of the place for days. The guide behind the counter looked worried.

'I'm not sure that Monsieur Martin is available, madame.'

'I'm quite sure he will be when he knows who it is. Would you be kind enough to let him know that Miss Nell Bray will be ready and waiting for him outside the Pension de la Gare at five o'clock tomorrow morning?'

He blinked, swallowed and said he'd do his best. I was aware of suppressed laughter around me at my high-handedness. With any luck this would be the talk of the town.

'And a porter, madame?'

I nodded grandly. I didn't in the least need a porter, but the insistence on one guide and porter per climber was one of the regulations that made climbing such an expensive business. At least I could afford it, on Beatrice's money. As I left the office the talk and laughter were breaking out behind me. I only hoped Pierre had kept his promise and come down the mountain in time to get my message.

My next stop was the office of Louis Veyrat. He came out from behind his desk accusingly.

'Have you been trying to make a fool of me? That linen sachet you gave me – the analyst's report has been telegraphed from Lyons.'

'Yes.'

'It contained tea, madame, simply and only tea. Not a trace of *tue-loup* or any other poison.'

'Excellent.'

'Excellent?'

'Exactly what I expected. It goes a long way to confirming my theory.'

'And this business with the coffin, is that something to do with your theory too?'

'What business?'

'Some malefactor broke in and tried to open Arthur Mordiford's coffin. The seals were hacked.'

I said nothing. I couldn't blame him for being annoyed, but I couldn't risk telling him all that I knew or guessed.

'And while you're playing your games, my client is in prison.'

'Believe me, I'm as eager as you are to get her out. I'm just asking you to trust me for another forty-eight hours. How is she?'

He gave me a long stare, shrugged and decided to calm down a little.

'She's a proud woman. She will not let anyone, even me, see that she's suffering. She complains only that her room is not properly dusted and the salad is served without dressing. She waits. I'm not sure what for, but I sense that she's waiting for something to happen.'

'For somebody else to confess perhaps?'

He gave an eager, pecking nod. 'You know of something? If you do, it is your duty to tell me.'

'I've nothing to tell you yet. Two days on, I hope there might be something.'

'Why not tomorrow?'

'Because tomorrow I'm going up to the Grands Mulets to paint the sunrise.'

His look of pain at my frivolity disappeared when I added: 'With Pierre Martin as my guide.'

He asked no more questions, only looked at me for a long time and said, 'Be careful.'

Easyday hadn't said that, but then she knew that there were times when being careful got you nowhere at all.

I kept away from the usual haunts of the British that day, wanting to give gossip a chance to flourish without my constraining presence. A few people who knew me would be surprised by my sudden interest in amateur painting, but that would add to the effect. In the evening I ate stew and drank rough red wine in a workmen's café, then went back to my room in the pension and checked the nails in my boots, my ice-axe and Gregory's journal in its waterproof pack. It had been in my pocket while Monsieur Veyrat was telling me about the coffin robbery. After that, there was nothing to do but sleep as well as I could. A quarter of an hour before the appointed time of five o'clock on the borderline between night and day, I was on the steps outside, waiting for my guide.

At five minutes to the hour he arrived, not in the least grateful that I'd selected him out of all the guides in town.

'What is this? A joke?'

He was ready to climb at any rate, felt hat on his head, rope over his shoulder, but there was a defensive look in his eyes.

'I want to see where it happened at the Grands Mulets.'

'There's nothing there from thirty years ago. The ice

changes. Even the hut's changed.'

'Of course, but I still want to see it. Now, do you think we could start, please? I want to be there before the others arrive.'

'What others?'

The porter, surplus to requirements, was loitering a few yards away, with a second rope and a small ladder. The fact that this painter of sunrises was equipped with neither easel nor paint-box may or may not have surprised him. I wouldn't even let him carry my pack because it contained the journal, and now I'd had a chance to read it again I was even more determined not to let it out of my possession.

It was lucky that I'd got reasonably fit for the mountains in my first week in Chamonix because Pierre set off at a fast pace, probably expecting me to beg for mercy. When he saw that it wouldn't work he slowed down a little and we managed the first few hours and the long climb up to the Plan de l'Aiguille briskly but in silence. We didn't set up camp here, as the slower and more heavily burdened Mordiford party had done thirty years before, just rested for an hour before moving on to the more difficult part of the climb. Pierre sat on a rock, rope over his shoulder, one hand on his ice-axe, the very image of the perfect guide, except that this one was in a tearing bad temper with his client.

'I've told you all I know. There's nothing else.'

'I believe you.'

'Do you know what one of the other guides said to me last night, after I'd got your message? "Try not to kill this one or we'll be running out of English tourists." '

'Plenty more where we come from.'

This made him no more cheerful and he remained in a bad temper until we reached the ice, where we roped up and he had to start concentrating on his job. Even on a fine summer day the journey across the glacier to the Grands Mulets is no joke. Our route was much higher up than the point where Arthur's body had been found and Gregory had confessed to killing him, which I think was a relief to us both. We climbed steeply with Pierre leading a zig-zag

189

route through the maze of crevasses that glinted blue-green in the sun, so deep that it seemed that anything that fell into them would plunge straight down to the valley five thousand feet below like a stone dropped down a well shaft. Sometimes there was no way round the crevasses and we had to cross them. It was at this point that the porter came in useful. He was carrying the light wooden ladder strapped to his back and we'd lodge it across from one lip of the crevasse to the other, pulling it up after us. Once embarked on the ladder you moved steadily and didn't look down. At one point I glanced up to see Pierre's worried face looking down at me. He seemed to have taken the guide's tactless joke very much to heart.

'Don't worry, I'm enjoying this.'

Which was true up to a point, only I'd have enjoyed it more if I'd simply been out for the pleasure of it, without the shadow of what might be going to happen up at the Grands Mulets rocks. I envied the other parties, mostly out of sight behind great blocks and ridges of ice, only coming into view now and then as silhouettes roped together, plodding upwards against the sky, or heads and shoulders popping up on the tops of other ladders as I crested our own. It was mostly quiet apart from the scrape of nailed boots on ice and the rasp of my own lungs drawing in oxygen, but occasionally the air would be split by the whoops and yodels of some triumphant party who'd been up the mountain at dawn and were on their way back to the valley. It was, on that fine day, a well-populated glacier with half a dozen parties of various sizes and degrees of competence making the ascent. Once a small queue formed when we and a larger party chose the same route over a crevasse. The others were Germans, with four Chamonix guides. I noticed that the guides looked at Pierre and seemed disposed to speak to him, but he turned away and pretended to be checking something in his pack. As the other party went on its way he only said: 'It will be crowded up in the hut tonight.'

He was right. The three of us made very good time but when we got to the Grands Mulets rocks towards the end of the afternoon the hut and its surroundings were as crowded as a beer tent at a flower show. I'd been curious to see this refuge, even though I knew it wouldn't be the one where the Mordiford brothers spent the night back in 1880. Since then the guides and porters had carried up materials from the valley to build a new one that's almost ridiculously luxurious for something perched on a rock at ten thousand feet. It looks austere enough from the outside but inside are eight bedrooms, a dining room and kitchen, a resident caretaker and a woman cook. The price of dinner with wine and a bed, at eighteen francs a night, is enough to take away whatever breath you've got left after climbing up there and my Baedeker guide-book had warned sniffily: *Food and wine often poor*. But at least the dining-room, shared on that evening by about thirty people, had the same atmosphere that I remembered from more humble climbers' huts. We ate at a communal table under hanging oil lamps. The talk, in various languages, was all of mountains, with the edges of people's maps getting into butter dishes, bad jokes flying round about near-accidents on the way up and over it all the smell of well-exercised climbers, pungent sausage and woollen socks drying that brings on an attack of nostalgia in anybody who loves climbing. If you met it anywhere else you'd probably light sulphur candles and send urgently for the rat-catcher.

The only other women present were three cheerful Americans who'd already climbed in Canada and Norway and were set to finish their tour of Europe by standing on its highest peak. They invited me to join their party to the summit next day and it gave me a pang to refuse. I wish I could have enjoyed the atmosphere and the chatter more, but I was on edge and so was Pierre. As we ate I glanced round every time the door opened to check the new arrivals but by the time most of us had got to the coffee stage nothing had happened. Still, I overheard one conversation between guides that gave me hope.

'Did you see poor Alphonse at La Jonction with his Englishman? The fool tried to jump a crevasse. Fell in of course. Just as well the porter behind him had a good hold on the rope or that would have been another one gone.'

'Beginner?'

'Surely. From the way he was behaving it didn't look as if he'd set foot on a mountain before. If Alphonse has got any sense he'll take him back down before he gets into real trouble.'

'Not Alphonse. Pay him enough and he'll get a performing seal to the top.'

'That would be easier than some of them.'

There was no sign that the Englishman was somebody I was waiting for, but it sounded like it.

This was confirmed half an hour or so later when the door opened and a man practically fell in, followed by a grinning porter and guide. Derisive cries from his colleagues welcomed the guide, Alphonse, at last. While the back-chat was going on the guide's monsieur stood leaning on the back of the chair, hat drooping in his hand, dark hair damp with sweat. He looked up and his eyes met mine.

'Good evening, Miss Bray.'

'Good evening, Mr Mordiford. You were able to leave your urgent business in Paris, then?'

'I've finished my business. I thought I'd take a little climbing holiday. Like you, apparently. I shouldn't have classed you among amateur water-colourists.'

'No, but people are full of surprises, don't you find.'

Ben's great dark eyes were fixed on mine but he had to struggle to find the energy to talk. Seeing his exhaustion, somebody made room for him at the table next to me and pushed a cup of coffee and a slab of chocolate into his hands. He drank, nibbled and began to recover a little.

'What are you trying to do?'

He whispered the question into my ear, under cover of the noise round us. The Germans were singing a drinking song. Alphonse was telling the story of the crevasse in a local accent impenetrable to outsiders, the guides and porters laughing.

'Following up a theory.'

'What about?'

'A murder.'

'Which one?'

'Both. They're connected like two people on a rope.'

'Climber's or hangman's?'

'Which do you think?'

He didn't answer and finished the coffee and chocolate slowly. He was at the stage of tiredness when even eating and drinking were an effort.

'I'm trying to protect my sister. That's all I'm concerned about. You're not helping.'

'You can't hide things for ever. The Mordifords should know that by now.'

'What's left of us. Beatrice would say it's a family curse, like the House of Atreus. A bit above our mercantile station, wouldn't you say?'

His head slumped forwards.

'You'd better get to bed. Everybody will be up early in the morning.'

'Ah yes. Must paint the sunrise.'

He closed his eyes. I waited until Alphonse had finished his story then caught his eye and let him put his monsieur to bed.

The American women and I were given a small room to ourselves, near the main door. I think they fell asleep almost at once, but I lay awake listening to the outer door opening and closing and the whispered conversations between caretaker and customers as some of the latecomers trailed in, well after dark. The very last party arrived at what seemed like the small hours of the morning, but was probably no worse than eleven o'clock or so, considering that we'd all gone to bed early. As far as I could tell, straining my ears in the darkness, there were three of them, guide, monsieur and porter. They must have done most of the tricky journey up the glacier by moonlight or lamplight – possible with a good guide but not something you'd do unless you had to. They were scolded by the caretaker for planning their day so badly and inconveniencing everybody. Neither guide nor porter seemed to worry, but I heard the client murmuring his apologies. He murmured them, almost incoherent with tiredness, in English. That was what I'd been waiting for. I turned over and willed myself to get some sleep.

TWENTY-TWO

BEFORE DAYLIGHT I WOKE TO hear somebody moving about in the passage outside, the scrape of heavy boots then the main door opening and closing. I got up, trying not to wake the others, and struggled into the clothes I'd left ready the night before. When I went into the passage there were other early risers sorting themselves out, finding boots by the occasional flame of a match, talking in whispers so as not to disturb those still asleep. It struck me as the prelude to a resurrection, with corpses stirring underground and wondering if it were worth all the bother. But then I was in a nervy mood that morning. I knew the man who'd gone out first should be Pierre and I thought I recognised the English voice of at least one of the people moving around in the passageway. I hoped Pierre would keep to the plan. I'd told him on the way up what I intended to do and he'd been very reluctant about it, full of a guide's duty to keep his client safe above all.

'Just forget you're a guide for half an hour.'

'One never forgets one's a guide.'

I'd had to spend more breath than I could easily spare on the way up trying to convince him and I was by no means sure of him even now. I laced my boots, picked up our porter's coil of rope from the place where I'd left it near the door and went out.

Cold was the first thing that hit me. I'd forgotten quite how shrivelling it was at ten thousand feet before sunrise. I stood on the railed terrace outside the hut looking down at the white shimmer of the snowfield. There was a moon and although it would be some time still before the sun came up you could sense that daylight was not far off. The light of the moon threw smudged lines of shadow on the snow, warnings of hidden crevasses. At this point there was nobody on the snowfield that I could see. Another half hour or so and parties would be moving off from the Grands Mulets rocks, roped together, for the long climb to the summit.

'No sunrise yet.'

Ben Mordiford's voice from behind me. He'd managed to give his guide, Alphonse, the slip and was there on his own, new tweed jacket buttoned to the chin against the cold and ice-axe awkwardly in hand.

'Not yet. I'm going down to see it from the snowfield.'

He said instantly: 'I'll come with you.'

He knew nothing about climbing, so probably didn't understand what an idiotic proposal I was making, but even so it must have been a desperate decision for him to make. He followed me down the steps cut into the rock. After the first of them the dark bulk of the refuge and all the warm humanity inside disappeared from sight as if they didn't exist. I heard his heavy breathing behind me and his ice-axe clinking against the rock. I went slowly.

From daylight the day before I remembered the horizontal ladder placed over the bergschrund, the deep crevasse between the face of the rock and the snowfield. I helped him over it, taking his ice-axe from him while he climbed, handing it back afterwards when we had our feet on the snow. His boots were new too. He must have bought them specially the day before.

'I'm going to tie us both on to this rope. If I disappear into a crevasse, drive your ice-axe as deep as you can into the snow, sit down and hang on to the rope.'

Some hope of that. He'd have trouble keeping himself upright, let alone belaying anybody else. If Pierre was watching as he should be, this was the point where he'd be most tempted to intervene. It was a really lunatic thing I was doing by any climbing standards. I envisaged a brief and poignant inscription on yet another climber's grave down in the cemetery of the English church: *It was her own silly fault.*

When I'd got Ben tied on to the rope I set off across the snow. I'd have gone slowly and carefully in any case, but there was a double reason for it now. I felt the rope go taut and then slacken as Ben began to follow me. I turned now and then to see him walking in my footsteps about seventy feet away at the far end of the rope, clumsily. I'd forgotten to tell him to coil some in his hand to make things easier. When we were two hundred yards or so out from the rock I stopped and waited for him to catch up with me. Ahead of us the dents and shadows in the snow covered crevasses. They might be anything from a few feet deep to virtually bottomless, there was no way of telling. I could see the hut on the rock, its window glowing gently now that somebody had decided to light a lamp. But the rock below the hut was dark and it was impossible to see if anybody was climbing down it. If this was going to work, somebody should be. I glanced up the slope and there, a hundred feet or so above us, was a black shape that might have been either a rock or a man. It moved and I knew it must be Pierre. I felt a sense of relief, but not a very strong one because of the cold and the distance between us.

Ben was standing beside me, panting from the cold and the altitude, a pleading look on his face.

'It would probably have been very much like this when your father killed his brother. You can see how it could have been done. Even earlier in the morning than this, probably, with no chance of anybody looking out of the hut.'

'Yes.'

He stared at me, shaft of his ice-axe trailing on the snow, gloved fingers clenched round the top of it. The effort not to turn my head up the slope or back towards the rock was making my neck muscles twitch.

'It would be a much easier murder than poisoning Gregory was, don't you think? Gregory's murder of Arthur would be an impulse. The other one took planning and cunning, plus the ability to think fast and improvise. It really was amazingly skilful in its way.'

'Yes.'

He took a step towards me.

'I should stand still, if I were you. There are probably crevasses all round us. The puzzle was the motive, but I think you can tell me something about that.'

I glanced over his shoulder back towards the rock. Something was moving across the ladder over the bergschrund. I hoped it wasn't another guide coming to save us from our folly. Not yet, at any rate.

'A question of money, wasn't it?'

A figure was coming towards us from the rock, walking directly towards us and far too quickly for safety. Another fool.

'The tea-pot business was clever. Not just one false lead, but two, first that and then the Gentian bottle. If that hadn't been broken the case against Madame Martin would have collapsed. Your family really has piled up debts to her, hasn't it?'

'I'll see it all right for her.'

Ben mumbled it through stiff lips, the cold getting to him. The other figure was only a few dozen yards away and had slowed down, perhaps realising the danger of what he was doing. Ben, following my eyes, turned and saw him. His fingers clenched on the ice-axe.

'Don't move,' I said. 'Don't do anything.'

The other man came up to us. We could hear his heavy breathing and the crack of his feet breaking through the crust of frozen snow. When he was close enough I said, 'Good morning, Mr Tenby. Your cousin and I were discussing why Gregory was killed.'

He stopped for a second, looked at both of us, then came at Ben with a rush. Ben yelled, began to run clumsily downslope, then suddenly the rope that joined us was whipping away across the snow and Ben wasn't there any more, just a dark gash in the snow and the rope writhing away to the lip of it like a live thing making for its burrow. I flung myself face down on to the snow, struggling to make the pick of my ice-axe bite, but the rope with Ben's weight on it as his body went down into the crevasse dragged me faster and faster down the slope after it. Snow was in my eyes, in my open mouth gasping for breath. I tried to throw my weight on the adze of my ice-axe to make the pick bite, could feel the sharp pressure of it digging in just below my armpit and the rope tight against my stomach but nothing seemed to work and I knew I was gathering speed, heading head-first for the same gash in the snow that had swallowed Ben. When, against all expectation, the rush stopped it was with a suddenness that juddered every tooth in my head and a rasping sound like a saw on bone. Still stretched face downward in the snow I raised my head just enough to make out what was happening. The pick of my ice-axe had caught on something at last, probably a piece of glacier ice below the snow crust. I was perhaps thirty or forty feet upslope from the crevasse and there was no telling how long the ice or whatever had stopped me would hold, but at least the rope wasn't moving any more.

While this was going on I'd been conscious of Ben's voice screaming from somewhere, then silence. I raised my voice from the snow and called.

'Ben? Ben, are you there?'

In retrospect, one of the sillier questions of my career. Alive or dead, there was only one place he could be.

A muffled shout came back to me. I couldn't make out what Ben was saying but at least he was alive and conscious and, judging by the amount of rope that had run out, not very far down. If he was lucky he might have landed on a ledge or a snow bridge and he'd be all right as long as he didn't thresh around. With luck. Hector was standing there looking down at me as if he couldn't believe what had happened. I said to him, finding it hard to talk in more than short gasps:

'Sit down in front of me. Dig your heels into the snow and hold on to the rope.'

He seemed slow to get the idea of it but at last did as I told him. Once he'd taken some of the pressure of the rope off me I managed to get myself reorganised, wriggled into a sitting position, drove my ice-axe shaft deeply into the snow and took a firm grip on it. We should just be able to hold him until help arrived.

Even so, it needed the weight of both of us and I was furious when Hector took a hand off the rope and began to get up.

'Hector, for heaven's sake stay where you are.'

If Ben slipped off his ledge or if the snow bridge in the crevasse broke under his weight it would be more than I could do to hold him on my own. But Hector took no notice. He got carefully to his feet and began walking towards the edge of the crevasse where Ben had disappeared, prodding at the snow with the shaft of his ice-axe.

'Hector, don't be a fool. You'll be in there with him.'

Ten feet or so from the dark gap in the snow he crouched down on his haunches.

'Ben?'

His cousin's voice came trembling up in reply. Hector would probably be able to make out what he was saying, but I couldn't. In the circumstances it was probably a request to reach down a hand and pull him up.

'No,' I shouted. 'Wait.'

That would have been about the surest way anybody could have devised for getting them both in.

'Tell him to keep still,' I shouted.

Hector did no such thing. He said loudly, 'Why should we help you out? You killed your father.'

'No.'

Ben's panic-stricken cry came up from the crevasse clearly enough for me to hear.

'Admit it, then perhaps we'll help you out.'

I shouted to Hector to stop, but I couldn't do anything about it without letting go of my hold on the ice-axe that was Ben's only hope of safety. Ben was shouting something that I couldn't make out, then there was another scream and the rope jerked.

'Oh my God. I nearly went. My hand went through. Oh my God.'

'Admit it. Admit you killed your father and we'll help you out.'

Another scream, then sounds that came up to me as a low groaning from the crevasse, not recognisable as words.

'Louder. Miss Bray wants to hear it too.'

'Stop this.'

'I killed him. I killed him. I killed him.'

A series of rising shrieks.

'For his money?'

'For his money.'

The despairing wail came up the snowfield like the ghost of a long-dead climber. Hector straightened up and turned to me, an odd look on his face.

'You heard that?'

'I heard it, but . . .'

I could hear something else too, something that Hector was too excited to notice, the sound of boots cracking the ice crust above us. A few seconds ago I'd glanced up and seen that Pierre was on the move as planned, hurrying down to us, taking huge risks with every step in this terrain. He'd started as soon as he saw Ben go into the crevasse. If Hector had looked up he'd have seen him, but instead he knelt down in the snow, closer to the lip of the crevasse and looked as if he were talking to his cousin. No reassuring words, I was certain of that. I shouted again to Ben to keep still, as loudly as I could, but with no certainty that he'd hear me. As Hector went on talking there was another sobbing cry from the crevasse, more despairing than the others, and the rope was on the move again, going so tight that it felt as if it must snap at any moment or cut me in half, trying to drag me away from my grip on the ice-axe shaft, pulling me sitting through the snow with my feet gouging deep tracks in it as I tried to resist. I managed to keep my grip on the ice-axe but then felt that moving too. The pressure was too much for it and once that gave way there'd be nothing to keep me from being dragged like somebody on a ghoulish toboggan ride into the crevasse with Ben.

I looked down towards the crevasse and saw Hector standing up, ice-axe raised above his head.

201

'. . . have to cut the rope. Only way, or you'll go down with him.'

I shouted, but his ice-axe began its downward swing on the tight-stretched rope. How Pierre got there in time will always be one of the mysteries of the Alps to me, but he managed it. I was half conscious of somebody running past me then Hector and his ice-axe were shouldered aside, sprawling in the snow and Pierre was running back towards me up the few dozen feet that now separated me from the crevasse. I felt something slam itself into the gap between the tight-stretched rope and my jacket and the downward slide was suddenly checked. Arms came round my waist and a pair of long legs slid down on the outside of mine, for all the world as if somebody had joined me on my toboggan, but at least it wasn't moving any more. When we sorted ourselves out later I found that Pierre had simply pinned me to the snow with his ice-axe shaft as a kind of human belay, then added his weight to mine in the most effective way possible. Whatever it looked like it meant that between us we could hold the weight of Ben, probably unconscious now from fear and shock.

We held him there long minutes until a rescue party that had seen something of what was happening arrived from the rocks bearing a ladder. They were joined almost at once by the American women with their guides and porters and between them they managed to haul up Ben's unconscious body, wrap him in coats and blankets and lay him on the ladder as a stretcher. All the time this was happening, nobody had any attention to spare for Hector and at first he sat sideways in the snow where Pierre's shoulder charge had flung him, not moving. Then once we knew Ben was out and alive one of the guides looked down the slope and shouted a warning.

'The fool. What does he think he's doing?'

We looked where he was pointing. It was almost completely light by now and on the snow-covered glacier below us we could see a man running and stumbling, snow gliding away under his feet as he made for the valley thousands of feet below.

The best climber in the Alps would have been lucky to get down there safely on his own and Hector was far from that. Escape must have been in his mind, down to the valley first then perhaps over the border to Italy or Switzerland but he might as well have hoped to fly there as do it this way. If he heard our warning shouts he gave no sign of it. Then there was a cry from one of the Americans beside me, a groan from a guide and he was gone. The gash of a crevasse opened and he slid into it, snow pouring after him. I could tell from the way the guides looked at each other that they had no hope of a rescue this time.

Without saying much we took Ben back. As we manoeuvred the ladder across the bergschrund he opened his eyes and fixed them on mine.

'I didn't kill him. Hector did.'

'I know.'

Once they'd seen us safe, the American women and their guides went on their way up Mont Blanc. I found out later that they got there without any further trouble. In that fine weather it was an easy day for a lady.

TWENTY-THREE

IN THE EVENING, THREE DAYS later, Easyday, Pierre and I were sitting on the bench in front of her cabin, Bismarck stretched at our feet. Both Pierre and Easyday had been nagging at me about the risk and I was tired of it.

'He was a very clever man. How would I have got him to admit it? If he took the trouble to follow me out into the middle of a snowfield, not being a climber, it was a fair sign that he was desperate.'

'So he'd probably decided to push you into a crevasse and hope it looked like an accident.'

'I'd have taken a lot of pushing, and Pierre was up there as a lifeline.'

Pierre said nothing. He was still furious with me, which was understandable, even if I had given him the opportunity to become one of the guides' legends. His dash through the crevasse-field to rescue us would be a story in the valley for a long time. But so, alas, would be the tale of the two of us sitting in the snow with his arms firmly clasped round my waist. As a crevasse rescue it had worked like a charm and the other guides knew that very well, but the climbers' sense of humour is not subtle and Pierre was a sensitive man.

'But Benedict Mordiford actually admitted he'd done the murder.'

'Of course he did. I'd have admitted anything too, if I were hanging on for dear life down a crevasse, wouldn't you?'

'Probably.'

In fact, knowing Easyday, she was probably the only person who wouldn't.

'That was what Hector was relying on. He was always a quick thinker. He couldn't have known Ben would oblige him by falling into a crevasse, but once it had happened he knew how to use it.'

'What was the point? He'd have denied it when he came up.'

'But Hector had already decided that he shouldn't. It would have been very neat from his point of view, his cousin dead in a crevasse with me as a witness to Ben's confession. And he'd have managed to make it look as if he'd saved my life by cutting the rope.'

'A clever man,' Easyday conceded.

'All the Mordifords are clever. But it wouldn't have worked, even with Ben dead. There was something Hector didn't know.'

The journal was in the pocket of my jacket. I looked across the valley to the Glacier des Bossons, where it had all happened, took it out and opened it towards the end.

'That's the whore quote. When I saw the journal before Gregory put it into Arthur's coffin, that was the very last thing written in it. After you and I stole it, I decided to read it again. There was something else, something Gregory must have written before he put it in the coffin.'

I turned several blank pages then showed them a double page with writing. It was in the same hand as the rest of the journal, Gregory's hand, but in bright modern ink with a broad-nibbed fountain pen. A letter to a long-dead brother.

Dear Arthur,

Perhaps I have my superstitions after all, as if you'd come out of the ice to see how it all ended. You will be sorry to know that I have lived and prospered and the curse of Cain has passed me by until now. I think that would have annoyed you.

So it may be some relief to your frozen spirit to know this. I have lived to see my only son turn against me and my daughter give herself to a blackmailing embezzler of our own blood. I have lived my life and that which I have done won't be made pure, but then, unlike you, I never expected it to be.

I have, by the way, given you the credit of fathering Mademoiselle Sylvie Martin, which is certainly more than you deserved in that department. The Mordiford blood was always warmer in me than in you.

Ashes to ashes, ice to earth.

It was signed, with a flourish, *Gregory Mordiford. Chamonix, 1910.*

Easyday read, translating into French for Pierre as she went.

' "Blackmailing embezzler"?'

'Hector Tenby. He was in a position of trust in the family company. He'd been milking the funds and his uncle suspected it. This business must have seemed like a heaven-sent opportunity for him to get a hold over Gregory.'

'But how did he know Gregory killed his brother? He must have got there long before you did.'

'Of course he did, but remember he had several advantages. He knew his uncle was worried when the news about his brother's body came through. He might have known from family sources that Arthur had been climbing the year before, so he'd have spotted the ice-axe clue at once. Above all, he was familiar with Gregory's handwriting.'

'So his only mistake was in choosing you as an interpreter.'

'That wasn't a mistake at all. It was part of his plan. I could kick myself when I think how he was trying to use me against Gregory. He heard some silly gossip about my reputation as a detective and he used that deliberately to scare his uncle, tighten the screw. I should have been suspicious from the start.'

Pierre asked, from over Easyday's shoulder:

'Then what was his mistake?'

At least he was talking to me.

'Misjudging his uncle. I'm sure that when the four of you were up by the glacier he came out with his naked blackmail threat at last. Either his uncle should say nothing about his plundering of the family funds and let him marry Beatrice, or he'd tell the authorities about the murder. It must have nearly killed Gregory, but the amazing thing was he wouldn't give in. He thought fast as well. If it was either giving in to a life of blackmail and seeing his daughter married to a rogue or confessing to murder, he decided to call Hector's bluff and confess. He committed himself there and then by telling you and Ben. That left Hector only one course of action. He had to kill Gregory before he could get down the mountain and make the confession official.'

With his uncle dead, Hector might have reckoned on covering up his financial crime in the general confusion, particularly if he married Gregory's daughter. He'd have preferred blackmail to work, but he'd equipped himself for murder in case it didn't.

'He was refining the plan all the time. He slipped the *tue-loup* into the tea-pot while Beatrice and I were looking for lemons. Then I suppose we must credit him with some sort of conscience for not wanting to throw suspicion on Beatrice. He dealt with that by making sure that I seemed to drink a cup from the same pot. But the cup I drank had never been inside the tea-pot at all. He'd made a kind of sachet with spoonfuls of ordinary tea and a piece of his handkerchief and brewed it in the cup. Then just to increase the confusion, he made sure the bottle of Gentian got broken, so everybody's attention was on the wrong thing.'

I closed the journal and wrapped it in its waterproof covering. Easyday's eyes followed it.

'What are you going to do with that?'

'Give it to the examining magistrate.'

Madame Martin had been released, with apologies, two days before but there were still ends to be tied. I'd already had long sessions with Louis Veyrat and the examining magistrate and expected more.

Bismarck began barking and footsteps sounded on the path. A white-suited figure appeared below us, walking slowly.

'Benedict Mordiford.'

He'd been under medical care in his hotel ever since we came down from the mountain. His face was a mass of sticking plaster and partly healed grazes and his arm was in a sling as a result of a dislocated shoulder. He went up to Pierre.

'I can't shake your hand, but thank you.'

Pierre smiled and looked awkward. Ben, equally awkward, turned, found himself looking at the glacier, shuddered and turned away again.

'I don't wish to see snow and mountains ever again. I think I might settle in the South Seas.'

'I think they may have mountains there.'

'The Netherlands, then. I shall start a new school of Dutch painting. Shall we walk, Miss Bray?'

We went together along the path.

'I ought to apologise to you. When you followed me to Paris I thought you were in league with Hector. I was suspicious from the time he engaged you.'

'I don't blame you.'

'Hector had convinced himself that I was a fool commercially but I had my suspicions about the firm's money. That's why I had to dash off to Paris, to telegraph lawyers and such.'

'And the results?'

'As I expected. Hector had been bleeding us for two years or more. Gambling on the Stock Exchange, mainly.'

'That must have been another shock for Beatrice. How's she taking it?'

He took a few careful steps before replying.

'Badly. She had to know about the money and she's beginning to see how Hector used her.'

I decided not to tell him that it had been in my mind for a while that Beatrice might have been an accomplice in the murder. Two things had convinced me otherwise, one of them the care Hector had taken to get her out of the way while he attended to the tea-pot. As for the other:

'You know, the poor woman was convinced for a while that you'd killed your father. It wasn't kind to run off to Paris without telling her.'

'What could I do? I needed proof of what Hector had been doing. She wouldn't have believed it on my word alone.'

We turned back towards the cabin.

'We Mordiford men do seem to be a thoroughly bad lot, don't we? All except the sainted frozen Uncle Arthur, that is.'

I thought of the quote in the journal.

'I'm not sure that your Uncle Arthur wasn't the worst of the lot. What do you intend to do now?'

'Paint. There's still enough left in the family coffers to keep me in Paris for a couple of years. Perhaps I'll get Beatrice to run what's left of the business. Stop her brooding.'

Another few steps.

'You may like to know that we'll be paying the two thousand pounds the family owe Madame Martin. That's a debt of honour and I'm making it clear to the lawyers that it must be paid, whatever else.'

I'd never heard him sound so businesslike.

'They'll be grateful.'

I imagined them in their chocolate shop near the shore of Lake Geneva.

'It doesn't need gratitude. Besides, I really like Sylvie. I am allowed to like my half-sister, aren't I?'

We got back to the bench where Easyday and Pierre were sitting in the sun, talking climbing. Ben turned his back firmly on the mountains and addressed them both.

'We're burying Father and Uncle Arthur tomorrow in the English cemetery, then I'm taking Beatrice back to England. I've no intention of ever coming back to Chamonix so I don't suppose we'll meet again. Thank you. Goodbye.'

They wished him goodbye and *bon voyage*. I walked a little way down the path with him.

'What about you, Miss Bray? Would you care to travel back to England with us?'

I looked up at the mountains and the sky. As far as you can ever tell in mountain country the weather looked settled. Easyday had invited me to stay with her as long as I wanted. The fleas in her cabin were beginning to tire of the novelty of my blood and she was almost certain to be able to keep her promise and persuade Pierre to take me up Mont Blanc again, all the way to the summit this time. I believed that he wouldn't, after all, be too hard to persuade.

'Thank you,' I said, 'but I think I might stay on for a while.'

STAGE FRIGHT

Gillian Linscott

Edwardian London, and the fame of playwright George Bernard Shaw is at its height. His new comedy, a feminist reworking of *Cinderella*, stars the dashing Charles Courts and the wife of a marquess, Lady Penwardine, who is secretly in love with her leading man. Lady Penwardine – stage name Bella Flanagan – believes her husband's friends are out to disrupt the play's opening night and needs protection; a fear apparently well-grounded when the play is indeed disrupted and somebody gets murdered in the process.

Enter Nell Bray, celebrated suffragette and amateur sleuth, brought in to look after Bella and finding herself in the midst of a most perplexing mystery. A leading man with a tendency to hit people, a volatile actress who returns to the husband apparently intent on her downfall, and, at centre stage, a red-bearded Bernard Shaw, with no one at all sure what *he's* up to.

Stage Fright is Nell Bray's wittiest excursion yet, and perhaps her most dangerous . . .

'Suffragette sleuthess Nell Bray is a smashing creation'
The Times

'Engaging . . . lively writing, nice period touches'
Observer

HANGING ON THE WIRE

Gillian Linscott

Nantgarrew military hospital is not a popular place: people object to the methods of Freud being used to treat traumatised soldiers at the height of World War I, not least because Freud is Austrian and so held to be on the enemy side. Monica Minter, stalwart of the Duty and Discipline Movement, is of the opinion that all the inmates are plain cowards and that the hospital is a disgrace. And then someone begins shooting at the soldiers . . .

Nell Bray, suffragette and solver of mysteries, holds no truck with either Freud or Mrs Minter. Neither does she approve of war, but attempted murder is another matter. So when her friend Jenny Chesney begs her presence at Nantgarrew, she heads for Wales – and into a plot that thickens by the minute.

'Engaging . . . lively writing, nice period touches'
Observer

'Intriguing'
Sunday Telegraph

'Strong on period atmosphere'
Guardian

'Engrossing'
Evening Standard

SISTER BENEATH THE SHEET

Gillian Linscott

It is springtime in Biarritz – and playtime for Edwardian Society. But that fast and fashionable world is suddenly shaken by the suicide of a high-class prostitute, and by the extraordinary contents of her will. Topaz Brown, hostess to royalty, rakes and roués, has left her considerable fortune to the suffragette movement.

Nell Bray, committed suffragette but no stranger to Society, is sent to Biarritz to collect the money, and gets rather more than she bagained for. Plunged into the mystery surrounding Topaz's death, she soon finds herself drawn through the tawdry slums and elegant boulevards of Biarritz on the trail of a murderer – and thwarted at every turn by a high class courtesan, a respectable maid, a British MP and a fellow-suffragette with murder on her mind and a gun in her bag . . .

'An ingenious period whodunnit'
Philip Oakes, *Literary Review*

'Linscott delivers a disarming vote-winner'
Sunday Times

'Excellent . . . A fascinating tale'
Daily Mail

'Exhilarating . . . A jolly mystery in fun wrapping'
The Times

BERTIE AND THE CRIME OF PASSION

Peter Lovesey

'1891, the year I saved the Sûreté from obloquy.'

Bertie, Prince of Wales, is in Paris, a city which holds many attractions for him, not least the actress Sarah Bernhardt. It is she who informs him of a recent murder on the dance floor of the Moulin Rouge as the cabaret reached its climax, and she who is convinced that they are dealing with a crime of passion.

When the Sûreté arrest an artist for the murder, the theory of passion appears confirmed. Bertie is on the point of quitting Paris and abandoning the case when new clues emerge. Prompted by Sarah, he is able to identify the real killer and save an innocent man from the guillotine.

The master of the historical mystery has produced a *tour de force*, a royal whodunnit which is also capital entertainment.

'Lovesey regally blends the beastly and the blithe in a crafty period delight.'
Sunday Times

☐	Stage Fright	Gillian Linscott	£4.99
☐	Hanging on the Wire	Gillian Linscott	£4.99
☐	Sister Beneath the Sheet	Gillian Linscott	£4.50
☐	Bertie and the Crime of Passion	Peter Lovesey	£4.99

Warner Books now offers an exciting range of quality titles by both established and new authors which can be ordered from the following address:

Little, Brown and Company (UK),
P.O. Box 11,
Falmouth,
Cornwall TR10 9EN.

Alternatively you may fax your order to the above address.
Fax No. 01326 317444.

Payments can be made as follows: cheque, postal order (payable to Little, Brown and Company) or by credit cards, Visa/Access. Do not send cash or currency. UK customers and B.F.P.O. please allow £1.00 for postage and packing for the first book, plus 50p for the second book, plus 30p for each additional book up to a maximum charge of £3.00 (7 books plus).

Overseas customers including Ireland, please allow £2.00 for the first book plus £1.00 for the second book, plus 50p for each additional book.

NAME (Block Letters) ....

....

ADDRESS ....

....

....

☐ I enclose my remittance for ....

☐ I wish to pay by Access/Visa Card

Number ☐☐☐☐☐☐☐☐☐☐☐☐☐☐☐☐

Card Expiry Date ☐☐☐☐